NADIN

HALLIE and the BROKEN GHOST

TINY TREE

TINY TREE

First Published in 2024 by
Tiny Tree Books
www.tinytreebooks.com

An imprint of
Andrews UK Limited
West Wing Studios,
Unit 166, The Mall
Luton, LU1 2TL

For Nick and Felicity

My rhyme and reason

Chapter One

Hallie sighed dramatically. She looked out of the car window at the rain pelting down, watching as the blurry grey streets raced by. It was the start of the summer holidays, and it was already a washout. Hallie sighed again, even louder this time, just to make sure Mum had heard her.

"OK, Hals, I'll bite. What's the matter?" asked Mum, tapping her fingers impatiently on the steering wheel.

"Oh, you know, the usual," said Hallie. "I'm only being *torn* from my home and friends, for the *third* time, destroying my *whole entire life*. You know, nothing *important*."

Hallie huffed hot breath on the window – fogging it up – and drew a sad face, then she added a few tears just for good measure.

"Oh Hals… come on, please don't be like that. You know this is how I make money. I buy a house that's falling apart, I fix it up, I sell it and we get to not starve or go bankrupt. Yay, lucky us!" She looked at Hallie in the rear-view mirror with a strained smile.

"Yeah, yeah. I know. Food is important. Blah, blah, blah," said Hallie making a face as she pulled her arms inside her sleeves.

"I really am sorry love," Mum said quietly, her eyes soft and apologetic. "We only need to do this a few more times and we'll be set for a bit. I promise."

"You shouldn't make promises you can't keep," mumbled Hallie as she gazed out the window.

"What's that?"

"Oh, nothing," said Hallie, "It's just that… it would be nice if we could stay somewhere long enough for me to make actual real friends, for keeps." Mum nodded as Hallie stared sullenly at her scuffed green skate shoes. She untucked her arms and began picking at the frayed threads of her jeans and noticed that she had bitten all her nails down. *Probably from the stress of moving yet again*, she thought, then she shook her head as if to clear away the thought. To cheer herself up, she decided to tease Mum for a bit.

"Look I know it's hard sweethear—"

"Also," interrupted Hallie, grinning mischievously, "my education is *totally* suffering from being moved to different schools all the time. I mean, I can't even remember how many wives Henry the Eighth had, and long division… pfft!" she said, mimicking her thoughts going up in a cloud of smoke. "Surely, as a *responsible* adult, you know it would be better for me to stay in one school instead of dragging me around the country looking for cheap houses." Hallie tried her best to look serious and forlorn, but Mum was stifling a laugh. Busted.

"Nice try, Hals, but you're the smartest kid I know," said Mum. "Your grades are higher than average, which they have been *every single year* and you know it. Though your acting skills could use some work," she grinned. "Besides," she said, her voice serious again, "I thought you were still talking to Hana. Isn't she a friend for keeps?"

Hallie swallowed, her throat clicking loudly, "Hana hasn't messaged me back for ages, Mum." She had been trying desperately not to think about the girl who had been her very best friend until Hallie had moved away, two houses ago.

"Did you try calling her?" frowned Mum.

"Yes," Hallie said, her voice sharper than she intended, "lots of times. She never picks up."

"Do you want me to call her mum? I could set up a meeting?"

"What, like a *playdate*? Oh please, I'm not five."

"Well, what about Nate, or Lottie from your last school? They seemed nice."

"Yeah, they *seemed* nice," said Hallie, irritably. She'd tried to forget about them too, "But *nice* people say goodbye when you leave; they remember your birthday and they definitely don't kick you out of group chats." Hallie could go on, listing the ways that she'd been abandoned and forgotten, but she was tired of thinking about it.

"Oh Hals, I'm really sorry… but maybe you need to be a bit more proactive. People move all the time and manage to keep their friends. Maybe it's *you* who needs to try harder," said Mum, trying and failing to catch her eye in the mirror.

"That is so unbelievably unfair!" said Hallie, her voice suddenly croaky as she blinked back the water that had appeared in her eyes. "It's not *me* making us move all the time!" Hallie threw herself back in her seat and crossed her arms over her threadbare Ghostbusters jumper as their old car bounced creakily over speed bumps. She sniffed a few times then, when Mum wasn't looking, she wiped her face with her sleeve.

Hallie glared at the back of Mum's seat, her stomach now a hot, tight ball. She squeezed her eyes shut then breathed in and out a few times until she gradually felt herself unknotting.

She opened her eyes and looked at the seat beside her where her magazines were scattered. Deciding that a distraction might help, she grabbed the latest copy of the 'Paranormal Press' and started flicking through the lead stories, snorting as she read the titles; *The Sneezing Spirit, My Baby is a Banshee,* and her favourite, *The Chupacabra ate my Guinea Pig.*

"Come on, hon," said Mum, far too cheerfully, "this new place will be great, I can feel it in my waters!" Hallie rolled her eyes, but she was relieved that Mum had changed the subject. "And I know how much you love exploring a new house, and this one is A-MAZING! So many weird little nooks and crannies to delve into. It's really old and creaky and you haven't even heard the best part yet…" Mum paused.

Hallie raised her bushy left eyebrow and put down her magazine. Despite her dark mood, she couldn't help but feel curious.

"Well…" asked Hallie, leaning forward in her seat, spilling her curly copper hair over her shoulders. "What *is* the best part?"

"Oh, I'm not going to tell you until we get there," said Mum grinning at her with a look that said, 'I can tease you right back.'

"Muuuuuuum! That's so *mean*, you know how much I hate waiting, eurgh!" Hallie flopped back in her chair and crossed her arms. She pretended to be annoyed as she stared at the moody sky but she couldn't hold in her smile.

"Wait, wait, let me guess," said Hallie, springing forwards again, "and if I guess right you HAVE to tell me everything, OK?"

"OK, sure. But you'll never get it."

"Right, first guess. Does it have a swimming pool?"

In response, Mum just stared at her in the mirror with an incredulous look, one eyebrow raised, then she shook her head.

"No swimming pool. All right then. Does it have a creepy hidden dungeon?" asked Hallie, practically bouncing in her seat.

"Hallie, yuck! No, it does NOT have a dungeon," said Mum, tutting but smirking as they turned left into a quiet tree-lined road. "Although I guess the storage could come in handy."

Hallie giggled, "No swimming pool, no dungeon. What kind of boring house is this anyway?"

"Hey, it's not boring!" said Mum, indignantly. "It's very, very interesting actually. Now keep guessing!"

"Does it have a…" Hallie tapped her lip as she paused to think. "Ooh, a cemetery?"

"No," said Mum, "I have not bought a church, but I suppose you ARE getting warmer."

Hallie took a sharp intake of breath, her eyebrows knotted and then her grey eyes widened, "Mum, please tell me you didn't…"

"Didn't what?" asked Mum, confused.

"Tell me you didn't buy a house where someone was…" then Hallie drew her finger across her throat, closed her eyes, stuck her tongue out and pretended to go limp.

Mum, who had just taken a mouthful from her flask, took one look at Hallie's face and snorted lukewarm coffee all over the dashboard. After a quick stop to wipe the car down and compose herself, Mum tried to pull a straight face; "No, Hals, as far as I know our house has never been the scene of a grisly murder – at least I hope not! Although I guess that might explain why I got it so cheap." She stroked her chin, "But now you're so close you're almost on fire!"

The rain had eased up when they finally pulled into a long and narrow gravel driveway, dotted with weeds and lined with shaggy bushes and untamed wild grass. She saw a sign, heavily rusted and swinging by a single screw from the worn gatepost. The paint had almost flaked off, but she could just about read it as they passed; *Ashbone House*. Hallie thought that this place sounded exactly like the kind of house where a grisly murder could have happened, but she kept it to herself.

"OK Hals, we're almost there, so you just have time for one last guess," said Mum, who started making a ticking noise.

"No pool, no dungeon, no cemetery, probably not a place where someone was offed… although I'm not so sure given the name," murmured Hallie. "Ha!" She clicked her fingers. "I've got it!" she cried, "It's *haunted*!"

The car stopped and Hallie clambered out, then she looked at the scene before her and gasped.

They were finally at the house – their new home for the next year – and it was the most hideous, broken-down, cobweb-covered horror film cliché of a house Hallie had ever seen.

"BINGO!" said Mum.

Chapter Two

Hallie stepped through the front door and her whole body shivered. She could feel an uneasy prickling at the base of her neck and even her goose bumps had goose bumps. The thought did not escape her that this was exactly the setup for at least a dozen horror movies and she wondered whether she should just cut to the chase and run screaming from the building right now, just to get it over with. Instead, she swallowed dryly and walked in.

"Wow, this place is super creepy," she murmured. "Hey Mum, do you know anything about who's supposed to haunt our new dream home?" asked Hallie with her hands on her hips as her mum grabbed the piles of junk mail from the floor.

"Oh Hallie, it's not *really* haunted. Old houses like this creak a lot, people hear the noises and make assumptions and the house gets a reputation, which is great for me because then no one else wants to buy it and I get it super cheap!"

"Uh-huh," replied Hallie, not buying her mum's explanation one bit.

"Oh good, the movers are here," said Mum as a large van pulled into the driveway. "Why don't you go and explore," she said as she scurried off to meet them.

The ceilings were high and decorated with intricate carvings that would once have looked quite grand and imposing, but they were now covered with layers of grime and cobwebs. The floors were wood and tile which might have looked inviting once, instead the creaks and cracks told her that the house hadn't been a *home* for a very long time. The walls had holes, the wallpaper was yellowed and peeling and everything looked unpleasantly sticky. This house needed a LOT of work, but Hallie could see that once her Mum had worked her magic, this house would make a beautiful family home.

"But not for us," Hallie sighed. Still, it wasn't all bad, there was exploring to be done. She grabbed the box she'd brought in from the car marked 'Hallie's Bedroom' and walked upstairs. *Time for bedroom shopping*, she thought. Hallie and her mum had a deal; Mum could haul Hallie from house to house and make her live in a perpetual building site and in return Hallie got to choose *whichever* bedroom she liked, no questions asked. It was really the only perk.

"Wow, look at this place," muttered Hallie as she wandered slowly from empty room to empty room, avoiding the higgledy-piggledy floorboards that seemed determined to trip her up.

Hallie walked into the first bedroom and looked around. The room was a good size and had a little tiled fireplace which she knew Mum would go wild for. There was a tiny pink sink in the corner with a big chip in it, covered in the same film of dust and grime that covered everything else. Hallie walked over to the window to look at the view and wrinkled her nose at the stacks of dead flies and spiders that littered the windowsill. "Fly corpses and a chipped pink sink, no thanks!"

The next room she wandered into had a large window, but it was so covered with filth, both inside and out, that it actually made the room look *darker.* A few of the floorboards felt suspiciously spongy and she worried that with one wrong step she'd end up falling through the floor and becoming the newest person to haunt the place, so she quickly left.

Walking into the third bedroom, Hallie was immediately hit by the smell of decay and rotting flesh. After being in so many abandoned houses over the years, while Mum scoped them out for sales potential, she knew the smell all too well. Covering her nose with her sleeve she tried to find the source of the stench. A quick look around revealed a maggot-infested bird in the huge stone fireplace and Hallie, though mildly intrigued by all things dead and decaying, thought the smell might be hard to get rid of. She ran quickly out when she felt her stomach starting to heave.

Finally, after poking around in the drab and shabby bathroom, she found the *best* room in the house.

"I hereby claim this room as Hallie's, forever and always," she announced to the empty space. "Or, at least, for as long as we stay here…" Then she pinned her homemade flag on the front of the door and set down her box.

Hallie appraised her new space:

"Biggest room… check."

"Huge windows which I can actually see out of… check."

"Massive scary-looking wardrobe where people probably hid bodies… check."

"Right, time to unpack!" she said cheerily to herself and began lifting heavy books from her box, handling them like they were old friends. 'Paranormal Britain', '100 Chilling Tales' and 'Ghost Investigations: Part 1'. She was just dusting off 'Ghost Investigations: Part 2' when she heard an odd squeaking sound coming from the wardrobe.

"Of *course,* the creepy noise had to be coming from the spooky wardrobe," said Hallie dryly. She ignored it and carried on unpacking. Hallie had just finished organising her box of books onto the built-in shelves when she again heard that weird squeaking noise, but this time it was louder.

"Hello… is anyone there?" asked Hallie. There was no response.

"No, Hallie," she said to herself in a mocking tone, adjusting her books on the shelves, "of *course* there's no one in your wardrobe. It's probably just the wood creaking as it responds to atmospheric conditi—"

SQEEEEEEEAK!

OK, there is ***definitely*** *something in my wardrobe,* thought Hallie as she froze to the spot, heart thudding too heavily in her chest. "I should probably check it out," she said loudly, in an attempt to scare off whatever it was, followed by, "I have a cricket bat…" Then she couldn't help but giggle nervously to herself at the thought of playing cricket with the horrendous gargoyle that was obviously living in her bedroom and quickly stopped when she remembered that her cricket bat was still packed away somewhere.

Hallie tiptoed toward the battered furniture with her arms stretched out and her face turned to the side to shield her from whatever horrid phantom lurked within. She looked like a lop-sided zombie.

"Easy does it. Nice and slow. Come on, Hals," she whispered. "Time to put on your big girl pants," which was Mum's favourite phrase. Hallie took a deep breath to steady herself and reached out towards the worn brass handle. She wrapped her fingers around it, the coolness of the metal pressed against her clammy hands and…

"HALLIE!" Mum shouted.

Hallie jumped and shrieked. Then she scolded herself for being such a wuss. "Coming!" she said, then bounded out of the room so fast that she didn't see the wardrobe door slowly opening behind her.

Hallie joined her mum at the front door. The rain had stopped and the smell from outside was green and fresh compared with the stale, stuffy air inside. A small girl stood in the doorway, a bike lay on its side beside her and she was holding a stack of papers and peering inside the hallway. Her dark hair was tied in a high ponytail and a thick fringe covered her forehead. The small girl's inquisitive brown eyes flicked across Hallie's face then she grinned widely.

"Hallie, this is Mila Cumisky, she was just delivering a leaflet for her family's business. Mila goes to Northpoint School too, she can tell you all about it," explained Mum.

Just then a loud crash came from the kitchen, followed by a string of unsavoury words.

"Excuse me," said Mum, who ran off to see what remained of her crockery.

"Hi," said Hallie, giving a brief wave to the girl who was craning her neck eagerly to see the inside of the house. "Did you… want to come in?"

"Oh no, no, no, no, nuh-uh absolutely no way," said Mila, who then blushed when she realised how rude she'd just been. "I'm sorry, it's just…" her voice lowered to a whisper. "You know your house is haunted, right?"

Hallie nodded, "Yeah I know," she said, "Mum told me the rumour. Though she doesn't actually believe it."

Mila's eyes widened in disbelief, "Wait, so you… you don't mind living in a haunted house?"

Hallie shrugged, "It's not like I have a choice, but it's kind of cool because I *really* love the paranormal. I'm a bit obsessed actually. I have all six volumes of the 'Ghost Investigations' series and I've binged 'Paranormal Tales' online," then Hallie chuckled nervously, suddenly aware that Mila was staring at her with her mouth wide open. "Yeah, I guess I don't mind."

Mila looked impressed, and then confused, "Para-what?"

"Para-normal," said Hallie slowly, "you know, ghosts, poltergeists, UAPs… that's what they call UFOs now; it stands for Unidentified Aerial Phenomena. It's basically just stuff that can't be explained by science."

"Oh! I get it. To be honest, all that stuff gives me the creeps. I can't even stand thunderstorms," said Mila, shuddering.

"So, er, what is your family's business?" asked Hallie.

"We rent out holiday cottages, we're just down the road actually. Here, have a look." Mila thrust a shiny leaflet into Hallie's hands. "We've only just opened up for bookings so Dad's making me deliver leaflets."

"But surely if the people around here already live here then…"

"Oh yeah, we're not expecting the people that live here to stay in them, *obviously*," Mila scoffed, "but they might tell other people about them. Word of mouth Dad calls it."

Hallie winced as another loud thumping noise came from the kitchen and she heard her mum groaning. "Cool, cool. So, um…" Hallie pulled at her sleeves, then flicked her eyes up to meet Mila's. "What exactly have you heard about the house being… you know, haunted?"

"Well," said Mila, eyes gleaming as she leaned closer, "when the house was abandoned, people would come here to snoop around, looking in through the windows and stuff, and they would hear weird noises coming from inside, even though all the doors and windows were locked."

"What kind of noises?" asked Hallie, her voice dropping to a whisper.

"Groans, squeaks, something that sounded like a trumpet… you know, not the normal creaky old house sounds, *weird* stuff." Hallie nodded, thinking back to the wardrobe.

"Hey," chirped Mila, eyes suddenly darting uneasily around the hall, "I have to finish dropping off these leaflets, but I'll come and find you when you start school in September if you like. So, then you'll know someone and won't feel totally awkward."

"No," said Hallie, a little too forcefully. "I mean, um, thank you that's actually really nice but you don't have to do that. I've been to lots of new schools, I'm sure I'll find my way around," she continued while suddenly finding something interesting to look at by her feet.

"Oh, uh OK," said Mila blushing, "I guess you can just let me know if you change your mind. Well, I'd better get going."

"Yeah, I'll see you around," Hallie said, cheeks burning as the girl rode off.

Mila looked hopefully over her shoulder, "Bye, Ghost Girl!"

Chapter Three

Hallie watched Mila ride down the bumpy driveway. She felt bad for rejecting Mila's offer, especially as she had been so kind and welcoming. Then she remembered the 'friends' she had made in all the other places she'd lived and how quickly their messages had stopped once she'd moved away. *No point making friends I can't keep*, she thought glumly.

Shaking off the thought, Hallie spotted one of her boxes, marked with bright red tape, stacked against the wall. She grabbed it and was about to head upstairs when she heard a quiet knock at the already open door.

"Excuse me, Miss," said a reedy voice, which echoed unpleasantly in the hallway, "are your parents around for a quick chat? I shan't take too much of their time."

A tall, gawky man with sandy hair and glasses that were far too big for his face awkwardly danced around the movers and hovered in the doorway expectantly.

"Hi… err, my mum is in the kitch—"

"My name is Edgar Dolos," said the man, cutting her off as he held out a fancy business card which Hallie had no free hands to take. "May I come in for a moment?"

"We're kind of busy right now, we're just moving in," Hallie replied, looking pointedly at the stream of boxes and furniture being emptied into the house. "Maybe you could come back tomorrow?" she suggested, now wincing from the weight of the box which was cutting into the insides of her elbows.

"I'll only be a moment," he insisted, "I'm a local historian and archaeologist you see. I heard you were refurbishing and I wanted to offer my services. I know a lot about this house, and I could help with any questions you might have; archaeological surveys and such."

"Er, I don't think… hey!" Hallie protested as he stepped into the cluttered hallway, pushing past her to get in and causing her to stumble backwards. Then, just as Hallie was about to shout, her mum's voice, calm and assertive, came from behind, "As my daughter just said, now is *not* a good time. Thank you for the card." Mum grabbed it from his outstretched hand.

"Oh," said Edgar, looking at Mum as though he had just tasted something unpleasant. "Perhaps I could speak to the *man* of the house?"

Hallie grimaced, *that was a mistake*, she thought. Mum's nostrils flared and she marched towards Edgar, forcing him backwards out of the house. "I will be in touch if I need you. Goodbye." Then Mum stood in the doorway and crossed her arms as though daring him to challenge her.

Edgar stood there for a moment with his mouth open before an angry expression briefly darkened his face. "Fine," he said, then he turned briskly on his heel and stalked off.

"What was *his* problem?" asked Hallie.

"Some people just don't like taking no for an answer," said Mum, "but you should never let anyone make you feel uncomfortable on your own doorstep," she added as she squeezed Hallie's shoulder, before returning to the kitchen.

Hallie, slightly ruffled by the rude man, turned to go back upstairs when she spotted her cricket bat sticking out of the umbrella stand. She'd started playing cricket in her first school but when she'd moved, and then moved again, she didn't have the heart to keep joining new teams. Now it just hung around to be used in case of burglars… or ghosts. She wrestled the box into the crook of one arm as she grabbed the bat and slung it on top.

Back in her cluttered room, in which a bed, a chest of drawers and several packing crates had now appeared, Hallie started emptying her box. She had done a LOT of packing and unpacking over the last few years, and she felt she could now do it blindfolded, upside down and in her sleep. She'd just finished filling up her sock drawer when a loud BANG came from the wardrobe.

Hallie gritted her teeth, refusing to turn around. *It's probably just the movers dropping something expensive*, she thought, not convincing herself at all.

There was something familiar and soothing about putting her old things away in a new house, stamping it with her own mark, and she was determined to carry on with her routine – even if it meant unpacking through an earthquake, hurricane or skeleton zombie apocalypse.

She took a framed photo from the box and lingered for a moment on the faces of two girls, arms slung around each other's shoulders and grinning. Her and Hana. A heat began to rise in her cheeks as she remembered sitting in her room with Hana as she promised Hallie that she'd video call her every night after she left. She crammed the picture into the back of her drawer and slammed it shut. Hallie had tried to throw it out several times, putting it in the wastepaper bin and then fetching it out again because she could never quite let it go.

Hallie sighed and began to unpack her extensive collection of ghost-themed snow globes when the wardrobe door opened by itself with a loud CREEEEEEEAK. *OK, that didn't just happen*, Hallie thought, trying her best to ignore the glaringly obvious fact that it definitely did just happen. As if answering her thoughts, the door opened just a little more and Hallie's stomach flip-flopped like she'd just eaten a five-day-old takeaway.

I'll just go and close it, it's totally fine, nothing will happen, she thought, ignoring the quiver in her inner voice.

Hallie began to walk slowly towards the wardrobe. What she wanted to do was to run screaming out of the house because even though she loved all things ghostly, she'd never actually encountered one before and the thought of being this close to an actual apparition was making her tremble. She felt a gnawing disappointment in herself. She, who has pored endlessly over magazines, lapping up details of terrifying tales, couldn't deal with one teensy-weensy little haunted wardrobe. What a let-down. She really did want to leave immediately; instead she felt like she was being pulled by a tractor-beam towards her certain doom.

Noticing the cricket bat, Hallie grabbed it, holding it across her chest like a shield as she neared the wardrobe which was now shaking and vibrating like it was electrically charged. With each step the shaking got harder, but still Hallie couldn't seem to turn away. Her body felt like a lead weight and she was clammy all over.

Hallie was really close now and her hand trembled as she reached out a pale arm. She put her hand on the door and instantly pulled it back, not because it was hot but because it was so cold that it made her gasp. She reached out her hand again and achingly slowly began to push the door closed when…

SLAM!

The doors flung open. Hallie was hit in the chest and landed hard on her back with an "OOF!" forcing the air out of her. Her eyes bulged as she tried desperately to suck some air into her winded lungs.

Then she saw movement. Something was spilling out of the wardrobe and loomed large above her. The ghost of a man in a tuxedo rose up and then fell on Hallie, pinning her to the floor.

Hallie tried to call out, but her deflated lungs were still useless. Instead, she clawed the ground and scrambled backwards from under the ghost, blood pounding in her ears and gasping, but the ghost bore down on her, arms outstretched, with its black and empty eyes and slack mouth pulled back in a silent wail.

Hallie braced herself and finally took a deep breath; a scream had risen from the very tips of her toes and was about to be unleashed when suddenly, ***squeeeeeeeeeeak…*** the ghost took off and began flying around the room like a balloon that had been let go, with a high-pitched squeal following in its wake as it flapped around.

Hallie ducked as it swished past her, and then she watched, eyes bulging, as it got caught in the corner of the room and deflated completely with an unpleasant slapping sound. The ghost man crumpled and folded up like a dead spider on the floor and then groaned.

At first, Hallie didn't know what to do. The ghost wasn't chasing her, which was obviously good, but also there was a GHOST in her BEDROOM! A ghost in a *suit*! And she was pretty sure, judging by the awful smell that now filled her nostrils, that the ghost had just done one epic *fart*. It was absolutely ridiculous.

Years of reading Paranormal books and watching ghost investigation programmes had simply not prepared her for seeing an *actual real-life ghost*! Hallie stifled a giggle. She needed to giggle partly because that's what she did when she was nervous and partly because she was pretty sure she had just encountered the world's first farting ghost.

Then, with a look of utter humiliation on its crumpled face, the ghost guffed again. A really long squeaky sort – just like the noise she'd heard in the wardrobe – and she just couldn't help herself.

The laugh burst from her before she could stop it, like a fizzed-up bottle of cola that just had the lid removed. Cackles and guffaws spilled out until she could do no more than wheeze and gasp for breath. The ghost simply looked on, bemused.

Chapter Four

Hallie stopped laughing and cleared her throat. Her head buzzed and she struggled to think sensible thoughts about what to do next.

The ghost, whose crumpled face was scowling at her from the corner, was still slumped on the floor. It looked utterly miserable. *Doesn't mean it isn't dangerous*, thought Hallie. She shuffled over to the cricket bat and grabbed it, then she stood up and edged towards the ghost, holding the bat out in front of her. *I must be mad*, she thought, *people are supposed to run away from ghosts not hit them with cricket bats.*

Hallie leaned forward, holding the bat out at arm's length, and was just about to poke at it when it spoke, making her drop the bat which clattered noisily against the floorboards.

"Oh, you don't need that thing child, look at me, I'm as useless as a glass hammer," said the ghost, eyeing her with such a pathetic look that Hallie felt a twinge of pity.

Hallie opened and closed her mouth, unsure of what to do next. She wasn't expecting it to speak, then again, she wasn't really expecting there to be a ghost in her wardrobe. Eventually, she decided that he looked about as threatening as a paper ball, so it was probably safe to respond.

"You can talk?" asked Hallie.

"Yes, of course I can talk dear, how else do you think I achieve my ghostly wailing?" The ghost shuffled into a seated position and crossed its arms, looking at her expectantly.

Hallie smiled weakly. "I'm sorry for laughing at you."

"Oh, don't worry about it," he sighed, "I really thought I had you for a moment though." Then he stuck his thumb in his mouth and blew until his cheeks popped out and his whole body inflated again. Hallie stared as he hovered a foot above the floor. "That's better," he said, then he stared at Hallie and she stared right back.

His tuxedo was old-fashioned but expensive-looking and he had a wiry black moustache that curled neatly at the edges. His hair, or what remained of it around the bald spot, was smooth, dark brown and neatly coiffed. He reminded her of a Belgian detective she had seen on TV once, except he spoke with a posh British accent.

The ghost clasped his hands under his chin thoughtfully, "You know you did look scared for a moment back there. Tell me, did you *feel* scared?" he asked hopefully.

"Yes," admitted Hallie, "I was completely terrified actually until… you know, the *thing* happened."

"Well, that's something, I suppose," he said cheerfully, straightening his back. "One mustn't knock one's progress!" He started to drift around the room, looking at Hallie's furniture and peering into her boxes, exclaiming in surprise at her trinkets and clothes.

"Erm, excuse me," said Hallie, a little put out at him examining her stuff. "Who exactly are you? Was this your house?"

"Oh goodness, where are my manners!" he exclaimed, "I'm so sorry, it has been quite a while since I've had guests, though it's no excuse for rudeness. My name," he said, performing a deep bow, "is Gerald, but my friends called me Gerry." Then he stuck out his hand.

"I'm Hallie," she said, but as she went to shake his outstretched hand, hers fell through his and it felt like she'd plunged them it ice. She pulled her hand back sharply.

"I'm terribly sorry," said Gerry, looking embarrassed, "I do hope that didn't alarm you." He sighed heavily. "Even after all this time I still forget that I'm not really *here* anymore. As to your second question, no this wasn't my house. At least I don't *think* so."

"You don't remember?" asked Hallie.

"Not really. It seems that some memories completely fade away after you've passed while others are very clear," he said. "I suppose in death you cling on to the things that were most dear to you in life."

"So, if this wasn't your house, how come you're haunting it?" said Hallie, sitting on her bed. "And didn't you see any white lights calling you to the other side? Or family members come to meet you? Ooh, do you have *unfinished* business?"

"My goodness you do ask a lot of questions, don't you?"

"My mum says it's a sign of a curious mind."

"Sign of a Nosy Parker more like," muttered Gerry. He floated to the bed and hovered beside her. "Who knows," he shrugged, "one day I was at the opera house and then it burned down – that much I do remember. Then I appeared here. And no, I did not see any white lights, beckoning family members or holy choirs of angels when I died, and I haven't the foggiest why I'm still here."

Gerry turned to Hallie. "Now it's my turn to ask questions. What on earth possessed you to move into a dirt-trap like this?"

"Hey! This is my house, no need to be rude," said Hallie, feeling somewhat offended.

"Sorry dear," said Gerry, "but it's not exactly *The Ritz*, is it?" He gestured to the crumbling walls and cobweb garland. "More like the Blitz," he said and chuckled to himself. Hallie rolled her eyes.

"My mum renovates houses and then sells them on. She bought this one because it was cheap since it's been abandoned for ages, and probably because of the whole haunting thing too. Not that I mind, I'm really into ghost stuff."

"Are you indeed?" said Gerry, lifting an eyebrow.

"Yes, look at all my books on the paranormal," said Hallie, walking over to the bookshelves.

"Go on then, tell me what you know about ghosts," said Gerry, smirking.

"OK, er, there are different types of ghosts; poltergeists, ones that look like a fog, others that just look like a blurry spot on the camera..."

"Well, that's nonsense for a start," scoffed Gerry. "We are all the SAME type of ghost, but how clear and loud we are depends entirely on our mood. When we are happy we might be active and loud, and when we are sad we can be little more than a wisp. Next!"

"Um, ghosts prefer coming out at night—"

"Wrong again... et voilà," he said, gesturing to himself. "Ghosts just can't be seen all that well in the light given that we are rather transparent. What else?"

"Ghosts make cold spots, and you can't tell me that's wrong because I can feel it!" said Hallie.

"OK, well I suppose they got one thing right," said Gerry crossing his arms.

"So," asked Hallie, "what about... the *thing*?" she said, almost whispering the last word. "That wasn't mentioned in any of my books."

"*Thing*?" asked Gerry.

"You know the..." and Hallie blew a raspberry while pretending to waft from her bottom.

"You mean how do I blow off when I no longer have a working digestive system... or a bottom?"

Hallie giggled, "Yes, *that*."

Gerry frowned, "I can only imagine that seeing my favourite place in the world burn down before my very eyes with my friends inside was somewhat *traumatising*," he said. "I have reasoned that it is a nervous response."

"I get that too, except I just can't stop giggling," admitted Hallie. "Wait, did you say your *friends* were inside?" asked Hallie, her eyes widening.

"Yes, but don't worry, they were already dead!"

"WHAT?" asked Hallie.

"Relax dear, they were *ghosts*," explained Gerry. "A few of my very dearest friends and I haunted the old opera house, but then some wretch set fire to it and poof! No more opera house... and no more friends." He seemed to droop sadly, as he hovered over to the edge of the bed.

"But where did they go if they were already dead?" asked Hallie.

"I don't know. I looked for them everywhere, but they were nowhere to be found and so here I am; a lonesome old fool."

"I'm sorry you lost your friends," said Hallie. Then she scratched her arm absent-mindedly, "I sort of lost mine too."

"Oh, you poor thing," said Gerry. "Did they expire in a fire as well?"

"No, they just sort of… never mind. Anyway," said Hallie, changing the subject, "are there any cool ghost tricks you can do?"

"Well yes, of course, my dear!" and with that, Gerry disappeared with an audible 'pop'.

"Where did you go?" Hallie jumped up and walked around her room. She couldn't find him, so she walked into the bathroom to see if he was hiding in there and glanced in the mirror...

"BOO!" Gerry's face appeared where hers should have been, and Hallie yelped. After her heart had stopped slamming in her chest, she started giggling. "Wow, you got me! That's awesome."

"Yes, it is rather fun," said Gerry, his voice sinking as his brows knotted together.

"What's the matter?" said Hallie.

"Well, it's all well and good being a performing monkey," said Gerry, "but none of that matters because when it comes to what *really* counts, I'm afraid I'm broken."

"What do you mean?" asked Hallie.

"I mean, since the fire, I can't scare anyone. I can make noise and rattle furniture but when I'm face to face with a living soul… one I haven't been acquainted with," he said looking meaningfully at Hallie, "I turn into a flatulent balloon. And no one is afraid of a farty phantom." He floated into the bedroom and slumped against the bed.

"But everyone knows the house is haunted because of *you*. That makes you kind of scary, right?" said Hallie, sitting beside him.

"Not really. The house already looks haunted because, quite honestly, it resembles some kind of forsaken hell-mouth."

"Hey!"

"I'm sorry. The thing is I need to see *terror* in their eyes, I want to watch them flee in fright. Until I've sent someone screaming and running for their lives it's not proper scaring and what is the point in being a ghost at all if you can't even do that?"

Suddenly, Hallie knew exactly how she would make the most of her time here, "Gerry," said Hallie, determinedly, "I am going to fix you."

Chapter Five

Hallie sleepily opened her eyes and…

"Ahhh!" she shrieked at the spirit who was floating two inches above her face, "*Gerry!* What have I told you about personal space!" Hallie groaned and pulled the covers over her head.

"You really should take care of that snoring problem you know," said Gerry seriously. "You sound like a warthog stuck in a swamp."

"First you wake me up at the crack of dawn and then you insult me!" Hallie's muffled voice came from beneath her blanket. "Have I told you how much I enjoy your company? Honestly, you're such a delight," she said sarcastically, annoyed that her Saturday lie-in had been disturbed. She stuck her arms above the covers and waved them about, poking them through Gerry's head and chest to swoosh him out of her way.

"Come on, lazy bones," said Gerry, unperturbed, "I've been waiting for you to wake up for an absolute age and there are only so many times I can read your ghastly magazines. I mean honestly, who believes that the royal family are really lizard people?" he snorted.

It had only been a few weeks since their awkward first meeting and Gerry was still very excited about having someone to talk to after years spent alone. So excited that he'd completely forgotten how to be around real live people; for example, he frequently forgot that living people liked to sleep, eat and poop without an audience.

"What's the hurry anyway? It's Saturday," said Hallie, sitting up and rubbing her eyes.

"Well, for a start," said Gerry putting his hands on his hips, "HE is here."

"What? Already?" Hallie glanced at the clock before jumping out of bed and running to the window.

There he was, Edgar Dolos. Somehow, with a bouquet of flowers and a bottle of cheap wine accompanied by a smarmy apology letter he'd managed to convince Hallie's mum to let him conduct an archaeological survey on the house.

"It's to make sure we don't accidentally obliterate something of historical importance," Mum had said shrugging when Hallie had asked why she'd invited the pushy man into their home. "Plus, he did apologise and sent me those nice flowers." Hallie didn't buy it, he reeked of bad vibes and he'd been hanging around like a bad smell ever since.

They watched Edgar come into the house and then heard his creaky footsteps on the stairs. "Why is he coming upstairs?" asked Hallie. "I thought he was working in the cellar at the moment?"

"Why don't we have a little looksee?" said Gerry, smiling mischievously as he floated towards the bedroom door.

Hallie followed and they both peered through the gap. They watched as Edgar's head bobbed into view and Hallie realised from the odd way he was moving that he was trying not to make any noise.

What are you up to? wondered Hallie.

Edgar stepped onto the landing and looked around, then

he reached up and started fiddling with the smoke detector that Hallie's mum had fitted last week.

"Good morning, Edgar," said Hallie, loudly, as she swung open the bedroom door and Edgar jumped, quickly snatching his hand back and holding his arm behind him. "What are you doing with the smoke detector?"

"Oh, Hallie," he said, smoothing down a crinkle in his jumper and pushing his glasses back up his nose, "I'm just... checking it, for your mum, making sure the battery is working – safety first and all," then he gave a wide fake smile showing altogether too many teeth. "Anyway, I really must get going, lots to do today," he said as he turned on his heel and headed back downstairs.

Hallie walked back into her room and took out a little red notebook from her bedside table. Gerry floated over her shoulder and watched as she turned to the next clean page and wrote the date in her neat print, then added a note about what she had just seen.

Edgar messing with the smoke alarm.

"Here on a Saturday, doesn't he have a life?" pondered Hallie as she consulted the record book which they'd titled, 'Dolos' Dodgy Deeds'. "No offence," she said, nodding at Gerry.

Ever since he had been allowed back in the house, Edgar had been acting suspiciously; frantic whispered phone calls, lurking in places he didn't need to be, flicking through Mum's papers and now messing around with the smoke detector – and so they'd taken to keeping a record of his comings and goings; and there was far too much coming and not nearly enough going for Hallie's liking.

Hallie had even tried to search for Edgar online, convinced that he was running some kind of scam, but all she could find was a mention in a local newspaper about the opera fire, where Edgar had talked about how awful it was for the local community to have lost such a historic building.

Hallie added the time to today's entry. Edgar always came early, before the builders arrived and often before Hallie had got up, and when Hallie had mentioned this to Mum she'd simply shrugged and suggested that maybe he was an early bird. Only, Hallie didn't think it was a *worm* he was trying to catch.

"Come on, Gerry. Time to switch on invisibility mode!" said Hallie as she bounded down the stairs.

"Are you sure you wouldn't like to finally introduce me to your lovely mother? Today could be the day!" grinned Gerry, waggling his eyebrows theatrically.

Hallie paused and looked at Gerry sympathetically. "Gerry, we've talked about this. If we introduced you to Mum she would freak out and probably drag me from the house and refuse to ever come back. We can't afford that."

"But *you* didn't run away screaming," reasoned Gerry.

"My mum doesn't have the same interest in the paranormal as me though," said Hallie. "She's far too sensible and boring. She'd take one look at you and decide the house was a write-off and probably burn it to the ground."

"Charming," said Gerry rolling his eyes. "Very well then, if we must continue this charade..." Gerry disappeared.

Hallie had thought long and hard about letting Mum know about Gerry but decided that she already had enough on her plate, and finding out that Hallie had made friends with the ghost-in-residence could push her over the edge. Thankfully, Gerry's ability to become invisible at will was quite handy.

In the hallway Mum was busy laying floor tiles, so Hallie tiptoed around her tools, Gerry following invisibly behind. Mum shivered as he passed.

"Hals," she called, "did you open a window? It's freezing!"

"No, Mum," Hallie grinned, "It's just me because I'm so cool…"

"Oh, HA, HA!" said Mum, sarcastically. "Shut the window!"

"Sure thing," said Hallie, winking at Gerry, whom she could just about see as a subtle green shimmer in the doorway. "Oh, and Hallie…"

"Yeah?" Mum appeared at the doorway, covered in grouting, and stepped through Gerry. She quickly rubbed her arms. "Ooh, it really is cold in here. Anyway, I was talking to Mike Cumisky yesterday—"

"Who?"

"You know, Mila's dad."

"Why were you talking to him?" asked Hallie, sheepishly, she already knew where this was going.

"He gave me the names of some people that helped him with his business. But that's beside the point. Hallie, he told me you gave Mila the cold shoulder. Why did you do that? She seemed nice."

"Mum, you know what happened the last few times."

"Hallie, it might be different this time."

"No, Mum, it won't. It's *always* the same. It's great when I'm here, but as soon as I have to leave they bail on me," said Hallie, crossing her arms.

"Why don't you just give it a go? It'll be a lonely year otherwise," pleaded Mum.

"Please Mum… can you just leave it. I can figure things out on my own."

"But I could talk to Mila's—"

"Mum, I'm literally begging you," said Hallie as she dropped to her knees and began yanking at her mum's jeans while pulling the saddest face she could muster.

"OK, OK, but don't come crying and saying you can't keep friends when you won't even try to make any!" scolded Mum as she went back to her tiling.

"What was that all about?" whispered Gerry, making her flinch.

"It's nothing," she said curtly, then set about making herself some toast.

After breakfast, Hallie and Gerry had just left the kitchen when they heard Edgar shout, "Finally! Father cannot deny my genius now!" before bursting out of the cellar.

Hallie managed to duck behind a wall before he spotted her and then carefully peered round the door frame, holding her breath. Normally she wouldn't care if he saw her, but she had that same gut feeling she'd had since his arrival… that he was up to something and she didn't want to be caught snooping if he was about to do something that might prove her hunch.

Edgar's blue jumper was covered in dust and stone chippings and he was looking at some architectural plans on paper that looked very old and fragile. He started muttering to himself quietly, but he was also smiling; he was obviously pleased about something but Hallie didn't know what his father had to do with anything.

"Gerry," said Hallie, in barely a whisper, "can you hear what he's saying?"

"Hold on," he breathed, so close that she jumped. Frowning, she watched the shimmer move closer to Edgar, who absent-mindedly started rubbing his arms. After a few minutes, Edgar gently folded the paper and placed it inside a worn leather case, then he closed and locked the cellar door and slipped the key into his pocket.

"Where did he get a key from?" murmured Hallie. They only had two sets of keys for all the locks in the house; one which Mum kept in her handbag and the other that Hallie kept in a backpack in her room. Mum usually unlocked any areas that Edgar needed to access in the morning and then locked up again after he left for the day.

"Damned if I know," said Gerry, whose sudden reappearance made Hallie jump again. The power of invisibility didn't come without its problems.

"So, what did he say?" asked Hallie, keeping her voice low.

"Just a lot of gibberish really. Something about finally earning respect, needing to visit a hardware shop, and then some boring musings about the thickness of Victorian bricks," reported Gerry. "Nothing that screams 'I'm a bad man, plotting evil deeds' I'm afraid."

"A hardware shop?" repeated Hallie. "What could he want from a hardware shop that the builders don't already have here?" Then her eyes widened, "Maybe he's planning to bury some *bodies* in our cellar and he needs tools to dig up the floor!"

"Oh yes, because we don't have enough sledgehammers and spades," Gerry said sarcastically, looking at a pile of sledgehammers and spades left by the builders.

Hallie huffed, "Well I still think that he's planning something, and it's only a matter of time before he makes a mistake!"

Chapter Six

After Edgar had left to run some errands and there was no more sleuthing to be done, Hallie and Gerry turned back to the task of 'fixing' Gerry. She had spent a whole evening devising a step-by-step training plan to whip Gerry into shape, but so far, he hadn't managed to get past the first level.

"OK," said Hallie, walking into one of the empty bedrooms, "imagine I'm some random man that just stepped into this big, haunted house. I want you to try and make me jump. That's all, just a little jump scare, got it?" Gerry nodded and Hallie stepped out of the room giving Gerry a minute to conceal himself before stepping back into the empty bedroom where the dead bird had since been removed from the fireplace.

"Wow, look at this weird scary house," said Hallie, acting badly and waving her arms about dramatically. "I really hope I don't see a ghost," she continued as she creaked across the floor slowly, whipping her head about to look for signs of her friend.

The lights started to flicker and the shreds of fabric that had once been curtains seemed to catch an invisible breeze.

"Ooh look at that, the windows are closed but the curtains are moving – this place is well spooky," she added, looking for signs of Gerry's pale green glimmer.

Hallie felt a prickle beginning on the back of her neck and goose bumps raised wildly on her arms. Then she felt a tickle on her cheek, which was one of her very worst tickly spots, so she started to giggle, which then turned into a chuckle as she thought about the absurdity of a human being tickled by a ghost.

Just then Gerry appeared right in front of her. "Oh! Wait, was that it? Not gonna lie, it was a bit anticlimactic," said Hallie.

"No, that was *not* it," said Gerry rolling his eyes. "But I cannot possibly perform when you're giggling like a village idiot!"

"Well, you're going to have to do this under all sorts of circumstances you know," said Hallie. "I mean, what if your target is a circus clown?" Gerry stared at her; one eyebrow raised. "I'm just saying you have to be prepared for anything. You can't be too fussy," she smirked.

"If you're not going to take this seriously there are much more pressing matters I could be attending to," said Gerry.

"OK, OK. Sorry, Gerry, look I'll be serious this time, I promise," said Hallie, passing her hand over her face and setting it back to 'serious'. "Cross my heart and hope to… er, never mind. Right, I'll give you one minute to hide." Hallie closed her eyes as Gerry disappeared again and after counting out sixty seconds Hallie opened her eyes and continued to wander around the room, waiting for him to scare her.

A ghoulish howling noise started to come from the fireplace and Hallie felt a little shiver, even though she knew it was Gerry. Then the windowpanes began to rattle, only slightly at first and then more violently, the glass springing around in the old frames, sending dry flakes of paint flurrying to the ground. Just then the bedroom door slammed shut so hard that wood splintered from the frame, and even though she knew that Gerry was behind it all, Hallie's heart was thudding in her chest. The temperature dropped and the lights flicked off. Hallie spun around, seeing only the grey light through the worn curtains. Then she spotted a thin yellow line coming from under from the doorway. A howling gale was now blowing from the fireplace, whipping Hallie's hair about her face as the window frames sounded like they were about to explode. The noise was terrible, and Hallie struggled through the wind towards the door. She reached out for the handle and was about to grip it when the door swung open and Hallie jumped.

"Mum! Oh, you scared me!" cried Hallie, panting to catch her breath. The second the door opened everything had stopped and the light flicked back on. "I thought you were out," said Hallie, smoothing her hair down and smiling guiltily.

"I was," said Mum, "but my appointment was cancelled. What was all that noise just now? It sounded like an earthquake!"

Behind her, Hallie heard a distinctive squeaking sound. The same long trumpeting sound that she'd heard on the day that she arrived.

"Eurgh, oh dear lord, what is that awful smell?" said Mum, covering her nose with her sleeve. "It smells like something died in here."

"Um, probably just some bird rotting away in the chimney," said Hallie, gesturing to the fireplace. "You remember there was that maggoty one that was on the hearth?"

"Yes, right, well I'll have to get someone to clear out the chimney then. Just another job to add to the never-ending list," muttered Mum, who took a quick look around, her face a picture of disgust, before heading downstairs.

"Oh Gerry," said Hallie, turning around dismayed, "couldn't you just hold it in?"

Gerry became visible again. He was wringing his hands, "I'm sorry Hallie, but you know I get nervous around other people," he sighed. "I was just hitting my stride before your mother came in too."

Hallie gave him a sympathetic smile, "You really were, my heart was properly pounding, and the wind thing... genius. Anyway, it distracted Mum from the noise though so... good job there," she said, giving him a half-hearted thumbs up. "But I guess it also proves my point that I shouldn't introduce you to Mum yet. Look, we can keep practising but we might have to do it outside, that's all."

"Alrighty then," said Gerry, looking a little cheerier as they headed into the garden.

*

After several more tries, Gerry could not quite summon the same level of fear that he had achieved in the bedroom and so he had scared Hallie precisely zero times.

The problem was that Hallie had gotten used to Gerry's telltale shimmer and icy chill, and she had been hanging around with him so much now that she even had a bit of a sixth sense when he was near (that and all the hairs on her body, including those on her eyebrows and armpits, would stand on end) which made it nearly impossible to *genuinely* scare her.

Gerry had argued that every time he used his invisibility she jumped when he reappeared, but Hallie counter-argued that it wasn't proper scaring because a) she always *kind of* knew he was there, b) he hadn't meant to scare her and c) she hadn't screamed, run away with arms flailing or fainted, and so it simply didn't count.

"The problem is, *you* know I'm here," moaned Gerry. "Scaring only really works when it's aimed at someone who hasn't the foggiest that there's a big scary ghost standing two inches in front of their face."

"There's a big scary ghost around here?" asked Hallie looking around before breaking into a wide grin.

"Yes, yes, very droll."

"OK," said Hallie, "so then, I think we need to ramp it up a bit. I think it's time to go to level 2."

"I'm not sure I like the sound of that," frowned Gerry.

"It's simple," explained Hallie, "you choose a scare tactic you've practised on me, but you use it on some poor, unsuspecting victim. You don't want to terrify them though, we want to start small until you feel more confident and can... contain yourself, so you're just going to make them jump a bit."

"Well, I suppose that sounds reasonable," sniffed Gerry, "but who shall I scare?"

Hallie thought for a moment, then grabbed a pen and notebook from her room. She wrote a small list of people who regularly visited the house:

~~Victims~~ Practice Partners
Lynn, the post lady
Phil, the pizza delivery man
The lady that delivers big parcels (can't remember her name)
Mila
Any salespeople
Builders

"Actually, not the builders," said Hallie as she crossed them out. "Mum would never get the house finished."

"Also, not Mila," added Hallie, "she's already frightened of coming here and I quite like her. She keeps asking me to hang out, not here of course, way too creepy," Hallie chuckled as she tapped her pencil on the notebook absent-mindedly, then her shoulders drooped. "Not that it makes any difference…" she trailed off, gloomily.

"Whatever do you mean?" asked Gerry.

"Well, you've probably noticed that you're pretty much my *only* friend at the moment," said Hallie, secretly mourning the fact that her bestie was a dead, balding man in a tuxedo who spoke like someone from an ancient TV quiz show. "It's just pointless trying to make friends when I'll just have to say goodbye as soon as the house is finished. I've done it before, lots of times, and it sucks *every single time*, especially when the minute I leave they can't be bothered with me anymore," said Hallie, her voice beginning to quiver.

"Oh, you poor dear," comforted Gerry, who tried to put his arm around her shoulders but only succeeded in making her back go numb.

"It's OK," she said, gently shrugging him off, "I'm used to it. Besides, at least I have *you* to talk to now," she smiled. "Anyway, I've just had a thought about who you can scare," Hallie said, trying to take her mind off Mila and the whole moving mess. "Tomorrow is Sunday, it's pizza and movie night and you know what that means…"

Chapter Seven

It was just getting dark when Hallie saw the lights of the pizza delivery car swing into the driveway. She had convinced her mum to order pizzas with lots of sides, drinks and ice cream so that the delivery man would have plenty to carry, giving her just enough time to give her poltergeist pal a pep-talk.

"Right, Gerry, it's *go* time," she said. "Remember, you only have to make him jump a little. Stick to the plan like we practised and you'll be fine. You can do this!" Hallie smiled broadly while she gave him a double thumbs up.

Gerry took a deep breath, an action remembered from his living days which still seemed to have a calming effect despite him no longer needing oxygen… or having lungs. Then he gave her a terse nod, sank into the floor and disappeared out of sight.

Hallie scrambled to the window and pulled back the curtains to watch as Phil, the pizza delivery man, grabbed the pizza bag and stacked two small boxes and another plastic bag on top, balancing it all with practised ease. Then he ambled towards the door, pulling his phone out of his pocket and checking it with his free hand as he crunched across the gravel.

Perfect, thought Hallie, *he's not paying attention.*

Gerry was already next to Phil; from her vantage point, Hallie could just about detect the familiar shimmer in the air beside him and as she watched, Phil paused and looked up to see Hallie in the window and gave her a nod. Hallie gave him a cheerful wave back and smiled as Phil suddenly shuddered all over.

"It's working," murmured Hallie, excitement bubbling in her stomach as Phil scrunched his body up against the cold spot that seemed to come from nowhere. Phone still in his hand, he pulled his hat down lower and pulled his collar up around his neck to ward off the sudden chill.

That's not going to work, Phil, sniggered Hallie to herself.

She saw the shimmer glide in front of the distracted pizza man, who was now swiping at his phone enthusiastically and laughing at something he'd seen.

He's moving in for the kill, thought Hallie and then…

RIIIIIIIIIIIING RIIIIIIIIIIIING

Phil's phone started ringing; a very loud and obnoxious tone.

"Uh oh," said Hallie, as she watched him answer it. Suddenly Phil looked startled before putting his arm over his nose and the sound of a very long and loud "PFFFFFFFFTTTTT," reached Hallie through her open window. She dropped her head in her hands and groaned as she realised what had happened.

Poor Gerry, she thought to herself.

Phil dropped his arm and then giggled as he chatted to whomever had called him, as he looked around to see where the noise and awful pong had come from. Seconds later, he hung up the phone and the doorbell rang.

Hallie heard Phil telling Mum that she might have a sewer problem and then she heard Mum making a disgusted noise as the powerful smell hit her. The door closed. "Hallie, pizza's here!" called Mum from the hallway.

"Be down in a minute," shouted Hallie, looking to see if she could spot Gerry outside, but there was no need. A moment later Gerry appeared back in her room, slowly seeping through the walls and looking just like a puppy that has just been scolded for pooping in your shoe.

"Oh Gerry, you were nailing it. What happened?" asked Hallie. She already knew but thought he might need to talk about it.

"It was all going so well," he said, shaking his head sadly. "I was just about to make my move when that infernal contraption started making a horrible racket and… well, I got nervous and…" Gerry then made a raspberry noise and mimicked the bottom wafting. "I'm hopeless!" he wailed.

"It's OK," said Hallie brightly, giving him a comforting tap on the arm. "Look, this is still progress and there were always going to be hiccups along the way."

"Hiccups wouldn't be a problem," said Gerry, "hiccups would be a dream compared to this nonsense."

"You know what I mean," said Hallie. "Look we'll just try again another day. Now, why don't you practise your scary face and after dinner we can plan our next move."

The very next day, Lynn the postwoman provided the next opportunity to practise.

Hallie and Gerry waited until she had delivered the post and then he drifted behind her as she made her way back down the driveway. Lynn began to shiver, but she was a tough sort and used to all kinds of strange and unusual weather so she shrugged it off and started rooting through her bag for her next delivery.

Hallie watched from the window as Lynne paused on the gravel drive. Gerry took the opportunity to up the ante and Hallie saw his shimmer move around Lynne, slowly, swaying from one side to the other. The movement created a greenish haze that hung around Lynne like a feather-light cloak. Then Lynne rubbed at her neck and seemed to swat at an invisible fly before rubbing at her nose irritably, all while still rummaging around in her bag with the other hand.

Then just like last time, Gerry shifted slowly in front of her.

He's going to do it! thought Hallie, slamming her hands on the windowsill.

Gerry was poised and all set to reveal himself when…

"Aaaaaatchooooooo," Lynn had a sneezing fit while her hands were still tangled in her bag and she couldn't find her tissues in time. Gerry was blown to the other side of the garden, farting as he was propelled into the bushes, making him sound like an angry bee. Hallie stifled a laugh, crouching down in her room in case Gerry saw her.

A minute later Gerry appeared next to Hallie's bed, spattered with snot and thoroughly fed up.

"Hallie, I must say that I am just about ready to give up on this endeavour entirely," he sniffed unhappily.

"You just got unlucky, that's all," said Hallie. "I'm sure there must be something in my books that can help!" She started flicking through her bookshelf, pulling out book after book, desperate for some inspiration.

Gerry shook himself out like a damp Labrador, flinging mucous all over Hallie's room, before he flopped on the ground by the wall.

"It's no use," he groaned, "I'm completely and utterly useless. What's the point of being a ghost if I can't scare anyone? I might as well just sit here and stare at the paint flaking off the walls until the sun goes supernova and puts me out of my misery," he huffed and Hallie watched as he seemed to fade in and out, like an old untuned television set.

"You're not useless," said Hallie gently as she replaced her books and sank down beside him, "I'm sure that once you get over your fear, you'll be a brilliant scarer. People will be wetting themselves to get away from you in no time, mark my words."

Gerry slumped a bit further down then seemed to stare into space, "You know the only thing I was ever really good at was entertaining people," he sighed. "It didn't matter how nervous I was before I went on stage or how many pairs of eyes were watching me, as soon as I was under that spotlight all my fear just slipped away. And now look at me," he said, holding his arms out with the remains of the snot still glistening wetly on his sleeves, "I can't even scare the post lady. Pathetic."

"Wait, you were on stage?" asked Hallie. "I thought you only *haunted* the opera house?"

Gerry sat up and shook his head, "That was after I died there, dear. I died on stage in fact; it had been a brilliant show too and I was just finishing off the evening to make sure we went out with a bang. And that we did, though not quite the way I intended," he said raising his eyebrows. "Everybody was still laughing because they thought it was part of the act until I didn't get up, and then the screaming started. But the thing is, I rather liked the screaming," he added thoughtfully, "almost as much as the laughing actually. It's what convinced me to stay and haunt the place, to see if I couldn't get a few more screams."

"Were you a performer, then?" asked Hallie, then her eyes widened. "I bet you were a comedian!"

“Lord, no,” he snorted, “I was the compère.” He floated up and swished over to hover by the window, his arm curled in a dramatic swirl.

Hallie’s face was blank. “You were the what now?”

“The compère, goodness what do they teach you at school these days?” Gerry put his hands on his hips. “A compère introduces all the acts and gets the crowd warmed up with their witty repartee.”

“Re-par-tee?” repeated Hallie, confused. Gerry rolled his eyes dramatically, then said sarcastically, “Me talk, people go ha, ha, ha!”

“All right, no need to be rude,” said Hallie, “I’m not as ancient as you, remember.”

Gerry looked out of the window wistfully, “Oh, how I do miss the stage. I rather think I’d do anything to be in the spotlight again with all those keen faces turned to watch me, waiting for the acts to begin.”

And all of a sudden an idea, sparkling and perfect, formed in Hallie’s mind and she knew just what she was going to do.

Chapter Eight

It took about a week after the great snot disaster for the perfect set of circumstances to present themselves.

Gerry had been busy practising Hallie's big plan and he'd finally built up the courage to try again when, right on cue, an early-morning salesman appeared at the door. Hallie's mum was singing in the shower, the builders were working at the back of the house with the radio playing loudly and Hallie was standing by.

"Gerry are you ready?" whispered Hallie as she walked towards the door. He nodded and gave a thumbs-up. "Break a leg," added Hallie and watched as he faded into the wall by the light switch.

Hallie opened the door to a jolly-looking man dressed in a red tracksuit and bearing an uncanny resemblance to a certain festive father.

"Hi there, my name is Gareth and I work for Synergy Broadband. Here's my ID," he said, showing her a card with a picture of him grinning through his short white beard. "Are there any adults home that I could chat to about our very competitive broadband package?" he asked with a forced smile.

Hallie smiled broadly, hoping that she looked innocent

and not like she was luring him into a trap. "My mum is in the shower, but she should be down any minute if you want to come and wait in the hallway. She definitely said something about needing broadband," Hallie urged.

Gareth glanced around the gloomy hall, saw the rubble, piles of timber and tools and hesitated, but it must have been a slow sales day because he eventually decided to step in.

"This is a... err, *nice* old house," he lied as he took in the swathes of cobwebs and crumbling plaster that they hadn't managed to fix yet. He inspected a particularly nasty-looking brown stain on the wall from an old water pipe leak and stepped hastily away from it. The door clicked closed behind him and he swallowed loudly.

"Well, it will be when Mum finishes renovating it," chirped Hallie. "Unless, of course, the ghosts drive us out first..."

Gareth looked at Hallie's eager smile and cleared his throat. "I'm sorry, did you say *ghosts*?" he asked, his fake grin sliding slowly back into his beard.

Hallie took a step closer and leaned in, "Oh yes, you must not be from around here then. *Everyone* knows our house is haunted."

"Oh," said Gareth who was beginning to look a little flushed. He started unconsciously scanning the hallway for possible exits as he took a few wobbly steps backwards towards the door.

Haunted was the code word that Gerry had been waiting for; it was show time. He started by turning the hallway light on and off, on and off, on... and off.

"Dodgy electrics, eh? S'pose that makes sense in an old house like this," said Gareth, who was shifting uneasily from one foot to the other, squinting then blinking as his eyes adjusted to the changing light.

"Oh no," said Hallie, "Mum had them fixed already." She patted the wall where new plaster covered the electrical cables.

The door to the kitchen slammed shut with an echoing BANG!

Gareth jumped, but Hallie just stood placidly as she allowed a creepy smile to inch across her face.

"Must be a breeze that pulled it shut," muttered Gareth as he glanced at the front door and absent-mindedly wiped a sheen of sweat from his brow. "Look, is your mum going to be long?" he asked, checking his watch. "I can always come back tomo—"

The lights came on fully, flooding the hallway with a sickly glow.

"Er… timed lights?" said Gareth, grasping for any logical reason to stop him from turning and fleeing.

"Don't be silly," said Hallie, a little too sweetly, "it's far too early for the lights to come on."

The middle light started to flicker, then it grew brighter and brighter until it eventually created one glowing yellow circle on the floor. Gareth stared at the spotlight, suddenly transfixed by the flecks of dust swirling eerily within the yellow column.

"That's unusual…" he tailed off as he saw a shimmery shadow start to appear in the beam of the light. He brushed the back of his neck and shivered involuntarily. Then he started rubbing his sleeves, his gaze never wandering from the light.

"W-what… is that?" Gareth stuttered as the shadow started to form the misty outline of a human figure. He began stepping backwards as his whole body trembled while he watched the head of the person-shaped shadow where first one and then two blue eyes appeared.

At the sight of a pair of phantom eyes floating without the body they were supposed to be connected to, Gareth screamed, slammed the door open and fled.

Gerry and Hallie whooped and laughed as they watched the unfortunate man run down the driveway, arms and legs pumping as fast as he could push them.

"Victory is ours! All hail the conquering hero!" cried Gerry triumphantly as he thrust his arms upwards and did a mid-air spin.

"Yes!" cried Hallie, fist-pumping the air. "I knew it would work! All we had to do was distract him first, *warm him up* like you used to do at the opera house. And when you stepped into the spotlight and pulled the trick with your eyes… it was just perfect!"

Gerry grinned, "It worked like a charm, and all thanks to you, my dear. It was just like being on stage again!" Gerry said gleefully. "But you were brilliant too! You wouldn't look amiss on stage either and what a clever plan. Bravo, dear, bravo," he said, applauding her as she curtsied in her old jeans.

"But it wasn't all me," said Hallie. "Besides, I think we can safely say that you are WAY past level two now! You were amazing!"

Just as the pair attempted a clumsy hi-five (which Hallie had taught Gerry for such an occasion) they heard footsteps coming from the cellar which cut their celebration short.

"Quick, hide!" whispered Gerry, who disappeared into the wall as Hallie dodged around a corner as Edgar stepped out of the cellar whispering furiously into his phone before walking out and round to the side of the house, clearly in a rush.

"What's that scallywag up to?" muttered Gerry by Hallie's shoulder.

"I'm going to get closer and try to find out," said Hallie as she moved to the window to see where he had gone. When she peered outside, she saw him standing just to her left. She gasped and quickly shrank back, then dropped to the floor and crawled on her hands and knees until she was underneath the windowsill. As she peered at Edgar from the corner, she saw him look around, as if checking to make sure he was alone. Hallie listened as his words drifted in through the open window.

"Yes, Father, I'm *certain* I've located it this time, below the cellar in Ashbone… I know, but the opera house was a mistake, you see I thought… Look I've checked it out at the site and this is definitely the place… No, she's clueless, she's got no idea what she's sitting on… Tomorrow night, I'll make it look like an accidental fire, just like last time… I won't disappoint you again, Father, I promise I'll bring it home. I'll make you proud."

With that, Edgar shoved his phone into his pocket and strode towards his car, leaving Hallie slack-jawed and terrified.

"I *knew* it!" said Hallie as she began to understand what she'd just heard. "He wants to burn our house down!" Gerry reappeared beside her and she felt her usual shiver.

"Yes," said Gerry, "I think you might be right about everything. I'm sorry I ever doubted you. And what was he saying about the opera house? You don't think he might have…"

"Burned it down?" Hallie finished, "I absolutely do." Gerry looked at Hallie, then cocked his head to one side. "I've just had the strangest memory," said Gerry, scratching his translucent cheek. "A few weeks before the fire, someone started hanging around the opera house, sticking their nose into the archives. No one seemed to know what he was doing there."

"Do you think…?"

"That it could have been Edgar?" replied Gerry. "Yes, yes I think it might have been." Then he looked stricken, "That blighter burned down my beloved opera house to try and get at something that wasn't even there," he said quietly, his mouth drooping. "All my friends gone," he added, looking towards the window.

"Gerry, I'm so sorry," said Hallie, then she blew a piece of curly hair from her face. "Wow, I knew he was dodgy, but I didn't expect this. What could possibly be below our cellar that would be worth burning our house down for?"

"It must be something very valuable for him to go to so much trouble. The absolute rotter!" growled Gerry, then he turned to her and saw her eyes flash and her cheeks burning red. "Hallie dear, are you all right?"

"He's already destroyed one home, I won't let him burn down this one too," said Hallie, determined.

"What do you want to do?" asked Gerry.

Hallie took a deep breath and then grimaced, "We need to tell Mum about Edgar."

Chapter Nine

Mum bounded down the stairs with her hair wrapped in a towel, still humming the tune she'd been singing in the shower. She picked up the post from the mat and jumped as she turned and saw Hallie.

"Oh Hallie, you made me jump!" said Mum, gasping. "Why are you lurking in the doorway?"

"Mum, I really need to tell you something," Hallie blurted, "and it's going to sound stupid, but you have to believe—"

"Woah, woah, woah… Hals! I haven't even had a coffee yet!" interrupted Mum, groaning and looking longingly at the coffee machine. She walked into the kitchen, tossed the junk mail on the side and started rummaging around in the cupboard frowning. "Hmmm, I can't find my favourite coffee mug, have you seen it?"

"No Mum, I haven't seen it. Please, I HAVE to talk to you, like, right now."

"Can't it wait a few minutes?" said Mum, still rooting around in the cupboard. "You know I'm useless before my morning caffeine hit."

"No, not really," then Hallie pulled her best 'worried' face to try and convince Mum, which wasn't difficult because Hallie *was* worried.

Mum gave her a long hard look, "OK, you'd better sit down and tell me what's up," said Mum, ushering Hallie to a kitchen stool while she picked up a stack of unopened bills.

Hallie breathed shakily as she planned what she was going to say. "Mum, it's Edgar. Firstly, he's somehow got a key to the cellar—"

"Oh Hallie, is *that* what all this fuss is about?" said Mum, exasperated. "Hals, I gave him a copy of my key. Remember he was working on the cellar because he said there might be some damp in there? Well, it made sense to just give him the key so I didn't have to keep locking and unlocking it myself since he's coming and going all day."

"You gave him your key?" asked Hallie, incredulously. "He's basically a stranger! Anyway, that's beside the point. Mum, he's after something *under* the cellar… and, and he's planning to burn down the house tomorrow night so that he can get to it!" Hallie felt sure that she sounded serious enough to capture Mum's attention, so she was surprised when instead of being concerned, Mum's brow knotted and her face became stern.

"Hallie, what's gotten into you? I know he didn't have the best start with you but he has apologised for that, repeatedly. Edgar is an archaeologist, not an arsonist for goodness' sake!" said Mum, who then opened the letter she was holding and scanned it before cursing under her breath.

"No, Mum," said Hallie, standing up suddenly, "you don't understand. I heard him on the phone! He said he'd burnt down the opera house but whatever he wants is actually *here*, under the cellar." Hallie was desperately trying to stay calm so Mum didn't think she was overreacting, though her heart was pounding too hard.

Mum started to look angry then, "So, you've been listening in on his phone conversations too?" asked Mum with her infamous raised eyebrow. "Hallie Alice Collins, I thought I raised you better than that! That's a terrible way to treat someone that's just trying to help us."

Uh-oh, thought Hallie, *she used my middle name. It's serious now.*

"*Please* Mum, you're not listening, he's going to do something really bad and—"

Mum stood up too then, "REALLY Hallie, I am too busy for this; I have carpenters and plumbers coming today and bills coming out of my ears," she said, pointing at the stack of envelopes and sounding more and more irritated. "Please leave the poor man alone to do the job I'm paying a ridiculous amount of money for, and no more wild accusations. You cannot make assumptions about him based on snippets of a private conversation—"

"You don't get it!" snapped Hallie angrily. "He's going to burn the house down, tomorrow night! He already destroyed the opera house and, and... we could die, and you don't even care! Just like you don't care about dragging me round the country from house to house just because you can't stand the idea of getting a *normal* job because you think it's beneath you, even though we're broke!" Hallie stopped as she took a shuddering breath, her eyes filling with tears as her words hung heavy in the air.

Mum's face and neck were turning scarlet and when she spoke her voice was low and came through gritted teeth, "That's quite enough. I think you need to go to your room before you say something you really regret."

Hallie searched Mum's face, but she wouldn't meet her

eyes. Then Mum turned away from her, grabbed the rest of the mail and started making coffee, banging the kettle and coffee jar as Hallie stomped up to her bedroom and flung herself on the bed. She hadn't meant to say all that other stuff, it had just come tumbling out before she could stop it, but in a funny way, she felt better for it.

"That went well then," said Gerry, who appeared sheepishly by the door.

"Wmfgh ee mfoing mto oo?" asked Hallie, face muffled by her bed covers.

"I'm sorry, what was that?" asked Gerry. "I don't speak duvet."

"Yes, very funny," scolded Hallie, sitting up, "I said, what are we going to do?" She wiped the tears from her face and massaged her temples firmly, as though it might make her brain work harder to find a solution. Then she took a deep breath and blew out slowly until the world made sense again.

"Well, perhaps next time we tell your mum something that just happens to be a matter of life or death… or a personal attack on her life choices… we wait until she's had a coffee." said Gerry as Hallie replied with her best withering death stare.

"All right, all right. Look, if we can't rely on your mother for assistance and presumably the local constabulary would pass it off as a joke…"

"Constabulary?" asked Hallie.

"The police, dear, and as I was saying, if we can't get any help then we'll simply have to come up with a plan ourselves."

"A little girl and a farty ghost against a fire-starting psychopath… brilliant," said Hallie dryly.

"Come on, where's your fighting spirit, child?" asked Gerry. "Aside from me, that is."

Hallie giggled. "You, in a fight? What would you do? Insult them to death? Gas them with your toxic bottom?" Gerry pouted and glared at her.

"OK," said Hallie, "but we need to be serious; we need to come up with a plan but we *have* to be careful or someone could really get hurt or even… or even die," she added in a sombre tone.

Hallie took a moment to compose herself. She was starting to feel panicky at the thought of facing off against Edgar. "We're going to need more than just a little jump scare to drive him away for good."

"Excuse me, did I not just pull off a level eight scare which included both running AND screaming?" said Gerry indignantly, hand clasped to his chest.

"Well… maybe a seven," grinned Hallie.

"Phooey to your seven, I was magnificent and you know it!"

That evening, Hallie and Gerry brainstormed their plan to foil Edgar, which they called 'Operation Deadbeat'. They'd been at it for about an hour when Hallie had a thought.

"I wonder," she said aloud, "Gerry… you can go through walls and things, can't you?"

"Yes," he said cautiously, "although I find it rather grotesque phasing through dirty bricks and spiders. Why, what are you up to?"

"Well, Edgar seemed certain that there was something buried under our cellar, something valuable enough to burn our house down for. Although I'm not totally sure why he couldn't just dig it up," she said.

"He would need to practically demolish the thing with a sledgehammer or a digger to get beneath that, so I suppose it would be easier to dig up the cellar if the house had burnt down," said Gerry. "I mean, what's a few more bricks when the whole building is already rubble? Then he could take what he wanted without your mother suspecting a thing."

"Yes, that does make sense," said Hallie, nodding. "Maybe you missed your calling as a detective!" she laughed. "Anyway, back to my first point… do you think you could…"

"Go under the cellar and see what's down there?" finished Gerry, raising one eyebrow.

"Yes! Pleeeeeeease." Hallie said in her sweetest voice.

"Well, I believe you have a key, do you not?" said Gerry. "Why can't you go down there?"

"Because I can't get *under* the bricks, duh. But…" said Hallie, eyes suddenly bright with the thought of adventure. "I suppose we could *both* go down and have a look."

Hallie waited until Mum had gone to bed, then she tiptoed to the cellar and opened the door, wincing as it creaked. She clicked on a big torch and walked down the few steps into the darkness, shivering with the cold.

The cellar was damp, musty and thoroughly unpleasant. Hallie shone the torch around and then Gerry appeared in front of her, his face lit up like a ghoul. Hallie jumped.

"Gerry, you idiot!"

"Ha! I got you," he grinned.

"Right," she said, "start looking for anything suspicious beneath the bricks and I'll look above ground."

"Roger, Roger," said Gerry as he disappeared into the floor.

Hallie inspected every corner of the room. Little piles of stone chippings seemed to be concentrated in one corner in particular and there were deep scratches in the floor and on the wall as if it had been gouged by a tiny pickaxe. But there was nothing else to see.

Gerry slid back up through the floor and dusted down his tux. Hallie looked at him hopefully, holding her breath.

"I'm sorry to disappoint you but there's not much there, apart from a whole community of spiders; horrid creatures," he said grimacing. "There may have been a small box of some sort in that corner," he said, pointing to the corner with the stone chippings, "but I think it was just a piece of wooden post from the foundations."

"Oh, are you sure?" said Hallie, trying and failing to hide her disappointment.

"No, I'm no expert after all, but whatever it is, it's buried rather far down… you'd need some heavy machinery to get to it, or a fire would do it, I suppose. Why, what's the matter?"

"It was just a stupid thought," she shrugged.

"Go on," encouraged Gerry.

"Well… I was just hoping that there might be something valuable down there. Then we could sell it and maybe have enough money so that we didn't have to move again," she said sadly.

"It's a nice thought," said Gerry. "Maybe we can do our own research to try and find out if there really is anything down there, using that bright clackety box of yours?"

"The computer? That's a great idea," she said, cheering up as Gerry took an elaborate bow.

"But right now, we have more important things to worry about. We'd better go and finish our plans for *Operation Deadbeat*."

"Right-o," said Gerry who disappeared through the wall as she flicked off the cellar light.

Chapter Ten

Hallie took a moment to watch the colourful blobs swirling beneath her eyelids before snapping her eyes open. She hadn't slept well and felt fidgety and anxious. *For good reason*, she thought, as it was literally a matter of life and death.

The main problem was that they just didn't know exactly what Edgar was planning. Where would he set the fire? What would he use? When? Questions crowded Hallie's mind and she found it hard to focus.

Gerry and Hallie spent the previous day scouring the internet for various things to help with their planning, including weather forecasts; common causes of house fires; how to make a house fire look like an accident; emergency exits in case of a house fire; how not to die in a house fire and a bunch of other things that made her search history look like it belonged to a pyromaniac and/or homicidal maniac.

Hallie had desperately wanted to start searching for whatever may be hidden beneath Ashbone house, they simply didn't have the time there and then but that gut feeling was niggling again.

Unusually, Gerry hadn't appeared yet. Though after the last time, when Hallie had yelled at him for floating so close to her face that she'd almost breathed him in, he'd taken to waiting just outside her door. Hallie smiled at the thought. It was comforting to know that she always had someone to talk to who could quite literally appear at a moment's notice and would always be there because he simply couldn't go anywhere else.

Hallie stretched awkwardly and dressed in her lucky vintage Ghostbusters sweater before sticking her head out of the door. Gerry wasn't there... *That's strange*, she thought.

Hallie started to walk around the empty rooms whispering "*Gerry*," but there was no reply. No tradespeople were coming today and Mum was still asleep, so the house was eerily quiet. Hallie didn't like it. She crept downstairs, not wanting to wake Mum who would undoubtedly question why on earth she was wide awake and sneaking around the house at 5.30 am on a Tuesday, which was definitely out of character given that Hallie rarely got up before 10 am during the holidays if she could help it.

Hallie cringed every time she trod on a creaky step, which was pretty much *all* of them. As she reached the bottom she breathed a sigh of relief and then immediately knocked over an awkwardly balanced sledgehammer which clanged like a bell onto a set of spades.

Hallie cupped her hands over her ears and squeezed her eyes shut. When it eventually stopped reverberating, she listened in silence for the sound of Mum moving around upstairs. But no sound came.

"Phew," said Hallie. "Got away with that one!"

"Got away with what, dear?" whispered a voice in her ear and as she spun around there stood Gerry, wearing the most terrifying face she had ever seen.

His mouth was pulled back too far, almost stretching from ear to ear, revealing a gleaming set of shark-like pointed teeth. His nose was little more than two black holes in his sickeningly blue-grey face. His eyes were grotesquely large and only the whites were visible, with red rims and deep shadows beneath them. And then, to top it all, was Gerry's normal hair, complete with bald spot. In fact, if it wasn't for that Hallie might have thought he was a different, more horrifying ghost altogether.

Hallie let out a high-pitched squeak that threatened to become a scream but clapped her hands over her mouth once her brain had processed the sight and realised that it was just Gerry after all. She waited for her heart to stop pounding while she panted heavily and glared at him from beneath her copper curls.

When she had finally recovered and made sure that Mum still hadn't woken up, she hissed at him, "What did you do that for? You could have woken Mum up."

"Well, I had to practise and I couldn't very well practise on your poor mother now, could I? Aside from the fact that she wouldn't hear me through her snoring," Gerry said, matter-of-factly.

"Yeah, well… fair point," said Hallie.

"I got you pretty good though, didn't I?" asked Gerry, pointing to his grinning face which he had, thankfully, smushed back to normal.

"YES! I was terrified," laughed Hallie. "I might never sleep again… why didn't you tell me you could do that?"

"I didn't know!" said Gerry, who was spinning with delight at the discovery of his new skill. "There isn't exactly a handbook for these things you know. Just think, I've been missing a trick all these years. I just started squashing my face around and 'Hey Presto!' I look like a horror show. Who knew!"

"Can you do any other faces?" asked Hallie, excited at this turn of events.

"Well, I have been trying a few out… hold on a moment." Gerry turned around and started rearranging his face. Then, he spun around and Hallie almost gagged. His mouth had been pulled down to his chest and all that Hallie could see was a gaping maw filled with row after row of tiny, sharp fangs. His eyes peeked over the top of his lips, bulging from their sockets and his body had melted into a giant gob of pink jelly-like goo. It was disgusting… and brilliant.

"OK, I think I've seen enough!" said Hallie, who didn't think she would be able to eat jelly ever again.

"But you didn't even let me show you my pièce de résistance!" complained Gerry popping his face back to normal.

"Save it for Edgar," said Hallie. "But this is brilliant news, we're sure to send the evil toad packing!"

*

Hallie spent the day doing absolutely anything she could to keep her mind off Edgar and *Operation Deadbeat.* But no matter how many pairs of underpants she folded or how many times she rearranged the things in the bathroom cabinet, her mind kept slipping back to their plan.

What if Edgar wasn't scared? What if he had a weapon? What if, what if, what if. Hallie had vowed to do everything she could to keep her mum safe and protect the house, but so many things could go wrong and her head was swimming with terrible possibilities.

After taking a walk around the block to clear her head and sneaking a cup of coffee when Mum was wallpapering a bedroom (Mum would never let her have coffee; she said she was lively enough already), Hallie felt more focused. Their plan was good. Gerry's new face-changing trick would add an extra element of terror which, alongside his disappearing act, would mean they could catch Edgar off guard. It also meant that Gerry could keep an eye out for Edgar without being seen, sort of like a supernatural sniper. Yes, it would all work out fine.

Hallie ate little at dinner, making the excuse that she'd had a big lunch so that Mum wouldn't know that it was because her stomach was a big bundle of nerves. Then after channel surfing restlessly, Hallie told Mum that she wanted an early night and retreated to her bedroom.

"Right then," she said to Gerry, trying to sound braver than she felt. "We need to go over the plan one last time."

"Hallie, dear, we cannot look at the plan any more than we already have. We *know* the plan side to side, upside down and backwards," Gerry said.

"Yes, I know," said Hallie, irritably, "I just want to make sure, Gerry. I'll feel better if we can just check it again, OK?"

"Look," said Gerry kindly, "it's going to be alright you know."

"BUT WHAT IF IT ISN'T?" Hallie erupted, eyes suddenly filling with hot tears that she couldn't stop from spilling as she blinked and fought to regain her composure. "Someone could die," she said, almost in a whisper as she wiped her wet face with the backs of her sleeves. But it was no use, she needed to cry and the tears would not be stopped.

After a few minutes, Gerry floated over and sat by Hallie who was now sniffling on the bed. "Are you all right now?" he asked gently.

"Yes, I think so. I just needed to get it out of my system," she gave him a tight smile. "It's just… well it's a LOT. You know?"

"Hallie," he said softly, "in all the years I've been alive… and dead come to think of it, I've never met a more determined and brilliant girl. There's nothing that you haven't thought of or planned for and that's the truth."

Gerry hugged her tightly for a few minutes. His embrace was cold and clumsy, but his chilly arms were just what she needed to shock her back to the here and now.

"Just remember," he continued, "you're not alone."

"OK," she said, taking a deep breath and feeling her clear head return, "I think we're ready. Let's get this done."

Chapter Eleven

Darkness fell, and as Hallie watched the garden disappear into the gloom she heard her Mum creak up the stairs and go to bed. She saw the light under her door flick off, and while she waited for her mum to go to sleep she thought she might do a little research on Ashbone House to see if she could figure out what was under the cellar, but something odd kept appearing in the search results.

"The Hebonas Stone," said Hallie, who quickly typed it into her laptop. Several results came up, so she clicked on the first entry:

> *According to legend, the Hebonas stone is a priceless statue carved into the shape of a flower and infused with toxins and poisons of all the deadliest plants in the world. Its potency is said to last for a Millennia and it was possessed by kings and regents, passed down from generation to generation, until it went missing, never to be seen again.*

Hallie pondered this and wondered what connection it had to Ashbone house.

Is that what's buried under the cellar? she wondered. It would make sense that an archaeologist might want to tear a house apart to find a priceless artefact, but Hallie thought there had to be more to it. After searching through every possible word and phrase combination around Ashbone House and the Hebonas Stone the internet still had no clear answers for her and so she slammed her laptop shut in frustration.

After twenty minutes Mum's breathing grew deep and steady with soft snoring sounds; it was GO time.

Hallie changed quickly into her all-black outfit and tucked her hair into a beanie hat. She grabbed the only piece of equipment she'd need tonight and stuffed it deep into her pocket and after one last quick glance at her plans she whispered, "Please let this work," to the empty room before softly closing her bedroom door behind her.

Hallie crept downstairs in the darkness. She knew the house well now and could find her way easily using only the pale light from the landing window to guide her. She had memorised which steps creaked and groaned under her weight and avoided them so that she wouldn't wake her mum. If she did, she would almost certainly be sent back to her room and evil Edgar would be able to carry out his awful plan. No, it was imperative that she was as quiet as possible.

When she got downstairs Hallie went into the lounge, grabbed an armful of cushions and carried them into the study. She piled them up beneath the window, which she unlocked but made sure was pulled closed, and went back into the lounge where she sat, fidgeting on the sofa for an unbearably long time, listening to the echoing tocks and ticks of the clock in the hallway. She went over every inch of the plan in her mind, looking for things that could go wrong and considering the best solutions until, finally, Gerry appeared in front of her.

"He's here, walking down the driveway," he said softly. "He must have left his automobile on the next street so we wouldn't hear the engine."

"That's good," said Hallie, wiping her clammy hands on her joggers, "if he tries to escape he'll be running, so we'll have more time to stop him."

Gerry paused and looked at Hallie long and hard then said, "Hallie, dear, are you sure you want to do this?"

"What choice do I have?" responded Hallie. "Mum doesn't believe me and Edgar's so slimy that even if I called the police he would probably come up with some ridiculous explanation and worm his way out of it!" She flung her arms above her head irritably. "If I don't do this, he destroys our house and years of hard work my mum has put in to be here. Plus, all the misery I've been through so that Mum could move us around cheap houses would all be for nothing. So, there is no one else. It *has* to be us, Gerry."

"Very well," he said, with a nod. He placed his hands on her shoulders for a moment and gave her a broad smile. Then he turned and drifted towards the door, grinning mischievously with his arms spread wide. "Let the games begin."

Hallie tiptoed out through the back door, locking it behind her, while Edgar walked towards the side of the house. The fences had been taken down to give the builders better access so there was nothing to stop him from going wherever he wanted.

Hallie and Gerry had guessed that he would try and start the fire *inside* as it had been very windy for the past few days, and with more gales forecast, being outside might scupper his plan. They'd supposed that, once inside, Edgar would surely start a fire in the kitchen. Their research had suggested that it was the most common place for a house fire to start so it would be easier for him to make it look like an accident, just as he'd suggested in the phone call; plus it gave him easy access to escape out of the back door. Thinking like a criminal was easier than they'd imagined.

"But how will he get inside?" Gerry had asked when they were discussing how he might do it.

"Oh, that's easy," said Hallie, "he has a key."

"What? I thought your mum only gave him the key to the cellar?"

"The cellar key is a master key which opens all doors apart from the front door. It's why I was so annoyed at Mum; she basically told him he could come into our house anytime he likes."

Hallie was now poised on the other side of the old conservatory and she gasped imperceptibly when, through the murky glass, she saw Edgar's dark shape sidle around the corner of the house and look around.

"Come on, Gerry," she said under her breath, "where are you?" Then right on cue, she saw the shimmer, barely visible in the dark garden.

Gerry moved in behind Edgar and then he passed *through* him. Hallie watched as Edgar seemed to shake his head and rub his arms to warm up. It was already unseasonably cold outside, especially with the icy winds that had blown in from Siberia – some summer they were having – but the chill that Gerry created was different, like stepping into a freezer. For the plan to work, Gerry *had* to encourage Edgar to go inside by making it unbearably cold outside.

"Wait, you *want* him to go inside?" he had asked in alarm when Hallie ran through the plan.

"Well, yes. Look, I know it seems more dangerous but he can't escape so easily if he's inside," explained Hallie. "Plus, we can *control* the room then."

"But didn't the weather report already say it was due to be cold? And I thought we decided that he was probably going to go inside anyway?" asked Gerry, confused.

"Yes, that's true on both counts. But we can't leave anything to chance. We need to make him feel as uncomfortable as possible and get him through that door."

Gerry had congratulated Hallie on her planning skills, but really she was just terrified that something might go wrong. The horror house that she had weirdly come to love might burn to the ground, Mum's business could be ruined; or worse, Mum could get injured. She might lose Gerry or get hurt herself… there was just too much at stake here to miss any details.

Hallie snapped her attention back to the dark shape that was now walking slowly towards the back door.

"Come on, Gerry," she breathed, "just a little more." She watched silently as the shimmer appeared again and again, pushing through and around Edgar to create a vortex of ice-cold air that pulled his hair up into stiff little tufts and then, at last, he rummaged around in his pockets and headed for the kitchen door.

Hallie saw him unlock it and felt a wave of relief that she had been right about the key. Edgar stepped into the kitchen and as soon as he had closed the door, she jumped up and ran. Springing softly on the balls of her feet, and stepping only on grass to cushion her footfall, she silently reached the door and then locked it behind him using her own key. She had greased the lock earlier that day so that it would be quiet and sure enough, it didn't make a sound. Then she left the key wedged in the lock and Edgar with one less escape route.

Moving quickly to the front of the house, Hallie climbed in through the unlocked study window, falling with a 'PLOMP' onto the pile of cushions she'd prepared. She locked the window behind her, shutting off another exit, and crept into the dim hallway to the front door. It was shut tight, locked and bolted in three places with a rattling chain for good measure. *Good*, Hallie thought, everything was going to plan.

Chapter Twelve

Hallie tiptoed along the hallway, making sure to avoid the tools and lengths of wood that were piled by the walls in haphazard stacks. The door from the hall to the kitchen was ajar, just as Hallie had left it, with enough room for her to peek through the gap. Hallie was sure that Edgar would not see her from the dim kitchen so she settled herself behind the door and let her eyes adjust until she could see his dark form moving around inside.

With Hallie looking on from the door and Gerry in the kitchen observing invisibly, they watched as Edgar quietly dumped out the contents of his backpack onto the kitchen table. He began pulling things out of it: A torch, some gloves, a box of extra-long matches and a gas mask – the kind that covers the face with a clear plastic panel. Hallie watched as Edgar put the gloves on, walked to the fridge and took out a bottle of milk. *What is he doing?* she pondered.

Going back to his backpack, Edgar pulled out one last item… a mug. Even in the gloom, Hallie recognised it immediately, it was her mum's favourite, the one she had lost. Finally, Edgar began hunting quietly through the kitchen cupboards until he found what he needed: tea towels and a saucepan.

Hallie was trying to control her breathing to stay as quiet as possible when Gerry gave her a little chill across the arm to let her know that he was there, a signal they had agreed upon earlier since they couldn't afford any accidental screaming.

"It's just as we thought," he whispered. "At least our skills of detection are tip-top."

"Yes," said Hallie, "he is definitely going to use the gas oven to start a fire."

"The blighter has even got himself a gas mask."

"Of course," said Hallie sourly, "he doesn't care if he kills me and Mum, but he couldn't possibly put *himself* in danger. But why did he take Mum's mug?"

Gerry paused before answering, "Well, I can't be sure, but I believe he's setting her up so it looks like she's made a drink of warm milk in the night and then left the gas fire on."

"Wow, he really is evil," marvelled Hallie, disgusted that Edgar would not only kill two people for his own gain but that he would also make it look like it was *Mum's* fault.

Gerry went back to the kitchen where Edgar had now switched on his torch. It was propped up on the kitchen table so that it shone a circle of light on the ceiling where the smoke alarm's tiny green light flashed silently. Edgar stood on tiptoes then swiftly removed the batteries and tossed them in his bag where they landed, clicking softly against each other.

Hallie gasped, then covered her mouth as she moaned, "I forgot about the smoke alarm upstairs," she said as Gerry appeared beside her. "I didn't put any new batteries in. But I think it'll be ok. As long as we stop him before he starts the fire it won't matter anyway."

"OK, if you're sure. Now, child, are we ready to begin the next phase?" asked Gerry, who was finding it hard to stay still.

"Yes," said Hallie, sensing his nervousness, "you have nothing to worry about, Gerry. Just imagine there's an audience watching like we practised with the salesman. And Gerry..."

"Yes, dear?"

"Don't forget, you're not alone either." Gerry smiled at her and then disappeared into the kitchen.

Hallie scowled at the now useless alarm and returned her focus to Edgar, who was busy arranging tea towels over the gas burner on the oven. He made it look like they had been carelessly left draped over the hob, then he poured some milk into the saucepan, swished it around and drained it into the mug before immediately chucking the rest down the sink.

Gerry was right, thought Hallie, gritting her teeth, *he's setting Mum up and making it look like she drank some warm milk and accidentally set the house on fire.*

Finally, Edgar left the mug, the saucepan and the milk on the side by the oven. His nefarious set-up was complete.

Edgar, whose torch was still propped on the kitchen table, reached to grab the box of matches when the torch started flickering. Hallie watched anxiously as Edgar grabbed the torch, grumbling as he smacked it three times onto the palm of his hand until the beam was steady again. He rebalanced the torch on the table and moved to grab the matches when Gerry turned the torch off completely, leaving Edgar in total darkness.

Hallie watched as Edgar stumbled as he looked for the torch, but even in the gloom, Edgar managed to find it. He fiddled with it, taking the batteries out and putting them back in again as he cursed under his breath, but he found that it would not turn on again. Hallie strained to see as the exasperated archaeologist started groping around on the table to find the matches and, after a lot of fumbling, took one out and lit it, the match flaring brightly in the dim room. Hallie shrunk back in case he caught sight of her face in the crack of the door. If he knew she was there, things could turn bad very quickly.

Edgar turned away for a moment to put the matches back on the table and when he turned back Gerry's ghoulish face appeared right in front of him, terrible shadows playing on his face from the wavering match. Then Gerry puffed and blew out the flame.

Hallie grinned as she saw Edgar stumble back and hit the counter hard, gasping and steadying himself. She couldn't quite tell but it looked like he was trembling and his head was whipping from side to side to see if the ghost was still there. She hoped Edgar was scared. Gerry took the opportunity to give Hallie another status report.

"It's going well, he's spooked all right!"

"Brilliant! And it doesn't sound like there have been any… mishaps yet?"

"No, none at all!"

"OK," said Hallie, "I think it's time for phase three."

When the house was rewired, on Mike Cumisky's advice, Hallie's mum paid extra for a remote device that could control all the lights in the house. It would save energy and the lights could be set to come on when they were out to deter burglars. Hallie had thought it was a brilliant idea. Hallie now took the smooth black remote from her pocket and after pushing a few buttons she switched all the lights on in the kitchen, smirking silently as Edgar suddenly threw himself down against the cabinets.

Edgar's head spun in all directions as Hallie alternated the lights, flicking them off and on. Slowly at first and then faster and faster. While Hallie had control of the ceiling lights, Gerry started on the torch again, flashing it intermittently, and the kitchen started to look like a creepy disco.

He must be ready to run, thought Hallie, wondering why Edgar hadn't made his exit yet. But as Edgar was once again plunged into darkness, she instead saw him scramble back towards the table, grab the gas mask and slip it over his face.

"Unbelievable," said Gerry, quietly beside her, "I thought he'd have been off at the sight of me but it seems that we may have underestimated the slippery fellow."

"Yes, that's what I'm afraid of," said Hallie frowning. "I think you need to get back in there, it's time for phase four."

Edgar was breathing heavily into his gas mask and the combination of Gerry's cold chill and his hot breath was fogging up the inside. Hallie watched on, worried, as the tall figure lurched towards the oven and started turning the dials.

"Come on, Gerry," she said urgently under her breath, her teeth clenched together. Just then the torch flicked on again and rolled across the table, creating a bright white spotlight on the wall beside Edgar.

Edgar slowly turned back towards the light, his hand shaking.

Gerry quickly rearranged his face into the most gruesome mask yet and appeared in the beam of the torch.

His mouth ran vertically from his forehead to his chin, and from it protruded long pointed teeth sticking in all directions. Three giant, slimy tongues covered with pus-oozing blisters flicked disgustingly from between the fangs. His eyes were drawn back to the far sides of his head and within each eye were two red irises. Beneath them were an extra pair of eyes that resembled those of an octopus and from the top of his head spouted eight humongous black and hairy spider legs that twitched and flicked menacingly.

Hallie, who was watching breathlessly from the crack in the door, couldn't quite see the whole effect. But the enormous spider legs were pretty obvious and she waited in anticipation of Edgar's scream, preparing to jump out of the way as he fled the kitchen.

But the scream never came.

Chapter Thirteen

Hallie could tell that Edgar was looking directly at Gerry, but she couldn't understand why he didn't react. He didn't so much as flinch. She wondered if he was paralysed in terror and hoped he would snap out of it soon.

When Edgar didn't respond Gerry panicked and lost focus which caused him to quickly shrink back to his usual form and then become invisible. Finally, because he was terribly anxious and he didn't know what to do, he farted, particularly loudly and accompanied by an unbelievably offensive smell.

"Who's there?" asked Edgar, hearing the noise, then, too late, he lifted his mask to see an empty room and immediately scrunched up his nose against the offending odour.

Oh no, something's wrong, thought Hallie, who could just about make out what was happening from her place at the door.

Then Gerry appeared beside her, body drooping and unable to meet her gaze.

"I'm so sorry," he said hurriedly, "his gas mask was so fogged up that he couldn't see anything at all. And I panicked… and now I've ruined everything."

Hallie was just about to suggest they switch to plan B when Edgar flung open the door.

"GOTCHA!" he growled as he grabbed Hallie and clapped his hand over her mouth as she kicked and tried to scream. He dragged her into the kitchen and threw her onto a chair. She wrestled against him, but he was so much bigger and stronger than she was. He clamped her arms to her side then, using one arm to hold her across the chest and face, he pulled something else from the backpack with the other – a roll of silver duct tape.

Gerry watched, aghast, as Edgar roughly taped Hallie's mouth shut before strapping her arms and legs to the chair.

Satisfied, Edgar stood back panting as Hallie struggled against the tight tape. She was breathing quickly through her nose, her eyes wide, trying not to panic, when Edgar spotted the light control device sticking out of her pocket.

"Very clever," he said, sneering at Hallie who was frantically looking all over the room for any sign of Gerry, "I suppose you have a ghostly mask or two lying around here too. Nice try, Hallie, but I've come too far to fail at the hands of a nosy little girl."

Then he flicked on the lights and switched off his torch.

"You might as well watch as I do this," he said with a smarmy smile. "I'm pretty sure your dear mum will be snoring too loudly to notice anything anyway, and flawlessly planned criminal acts like this are so rarely witnessed. And to think…" he said, pausing as in if thought, "if you hadn't farted, I'd still think this lousy house was haunted and my plan might have been derailed."

Hallie made an angry noise in protest and then watched as Edgar walked to the oven and found the right dial. He switched on the gas and dropped his mask back over his face. Hallie began to panic. Gerry was nowhere to be seen, she could smell gas and she could barely breathe with the tape over her mouth.

"I can't believe your insipid mother didn't get a proper archaeological survey," said Edgar, slightly muffled by the plastic mask. "If she had, they would have found an irregularity in the floor of the cellar and maybe, if they were diligent, they would have realised that it was the final resting place of the legendary Hebonas stone."

Hallie's eyes widened.

"Oh, I see you've heard of it," said Edgar as he picked up the box of matches. Hallie nodded stiffly. "You're not entirely stupid and self-absorbed like most your age then," he scoffed, "but what you might not know is that the legend surrounding this stone suggests that it has a peculiar effect on people. If someone living touches it, they die. But if it touches someone already dead… they can live again."

Hallie's breath hitched.

"A stone that controls life and death would make me the most rich, famous and powerful man in the world don't you think? And so, little Hallie, I must bid you adieu as I burn down your house and claim my victory." Then he stopped and looked at Hallie, the serious expression on his face blurred by the condensation. "You know, if you'd just stayed in bed, you would probably have got out of this alive. You could even have saved your mum. But now you'll both burn because *you* decided to interfere. How funny," he said, chortling to himself.

Hallie writhed violently, rocking and bouncing her chair while trying to scream or make any noise at all as Edgar walked to the oven and got ready to strike the match.

Then Gerry suddenly materialised in front of his face with an audible 'POP'.

"NO!" he screamed at Edgar, who reeled at the sound. Gerry grabbed Edgar's mask, wrenched it off his head and threw it across the room.

He can move things? thought Hallie, confused. She'd seen him rattle furniture and windows, but he'd never been able to move objects across a room.

He must be angry, she thought.

Edgar shrieked as Gerry started to morph into his most horrific form, the spider legs sprouted, his toothy maw parted and the oozing tongues started flicking to and fro.

That, it seemed, was finally enough for Edgar. He screeched and dropped to the ground, pedalling backwards with his heels before his back hit the cabinets where he sprang up and darted round the other side of the table, with Gerry floating after him. But, just as Edgar was about to leave the kitchen he turned, eyes full of terror and hands fumbling with the matchbox.

Hallie could see, too late, what he was going to do and she tried to alert Gerry, who was still pursuing Edgar, with a strangled cry. But it was no use.

Edgar struck the match and threw it at the hob.

The whole oven erupted into orange flame and the surge of heat knocked Hallie onto her back, still tied to the chair. The lingering gas had been consumed by fire and now half the kitchen was alight, with undulating smoke rapidly spreading across the ceiling.

Edgar had fled into the hallway and was clawing at the bolts and scrabbling with the chain, but the door was still locked and he, and everyone else in the house, were trapped.

As soon as the fire ignited, Gerry swooped down to Hallie and using his still sharp teeth he tore apart the tape that was holding her to the chair. She pulled the tape off her mouth, wincing at the pain and then tried to open the back door. It was locked.

"Of course, I locked it!" she cried as she ran into the hallway, coughing and crying at the irony that she had left the key in the lock to trap Edgar but had only succeeded in trapping herself. Edgar was now throwing himself, shoulders first, into the front door to try and break it down, but he was no match for the solid oak that had stood for centuries. He saw Hallie and screeched, "UNLOCK IT!" but her keys were still in the kitchen door.

Instead, she started heading for the bedrooms, she had to get to Mum, but as soon as she began climbing the steps her chest hitched and she couldn't catch a breath. She was choking on the acrid stench of burning timbers and plaster and it stung her eyes so badly that she could barely open them. The smoke and heat were now pouring from the kitchen and up the stairs. There was no way to get through without dying herself.

"GERRY," she screamed, eyes now streaming and smoke filling her lungs, "YOU HAVE TO SAVE MUM!"

Gerry nodded and bellowed, "GET OUT!" as he flew up the stairs. Hallie knew it was a risk, Mum might be so scared of seeing a ghost that it might cause her to hide or do something stupid, but they were out of time and options.

Hallie dropped to the floor and crawled into the lounge, trying to cover her mouth with her sleeve while Edgar still hammered, coughing and spluttering, at the unyielding front door. She spotted a sledgehammer and dragged it quickly to the window, then using all her remaining might, she brought it crashing down through the ancient pane, sending a cascade of sharp fragments down upon her head and gulping in a welcome lungful of the chilled night air.

Edgar came running in when he heard the glass break. He pushed Hallie aside and, taking a running jump, he hurdled out of the jagged window and ran away up the driveway.

Hallie didn't care that he was getting away. She had to get out, she had to get her Mum out, but the smoke was so thick now that she could no longer see anything. She groped around and found a cushion and pushed some of the jagged edges out, then she half climbed and half dropped out of the window. She lay on her back for a few seconds, coughing and panting to expel the smoke and replace it with clean air. Then she scrambled to her feet and ran, as fast as her lungs would allow her, to the back door.

So far there was no sign of Gerry or Mum and her body was knotted with worry, but she had to create an exit for them. Hallie grabbed her keys from the kitchen door.

"Ow!" she immediately dropped them, her hand burning from the super-heated metal. Using her sleeve, she picked it up and raced back around to the front door. She fumbled with the lock, feeling the heat building behind the oak panels and, because Edgar had already opened the bolts and chain, the door sprang open as smoke flooded out.

Hallie threw herself to the ground, feeling the heat drying her skin. Her nose was filled with the smell of her own singed hair and clothes.

"MUM, MUUUUM!" she screamed, struggling to her feet and wavering from side to side as she searched the windows and the doorways frantically for signs of life. She sobbed in huge hiccupping gasps as she realised that her Mum was going to die, and it was all her fault.

She could see angry flames climbing the side of the house and black clouds billowing from every exit.

Then Hallie gasped as she heard the most wonderful sound… sirens.

Chapter Fourteen

Three fire engines screeched into the driveway, sending the shingle flying as they lined up and the firefighters began to jump down and unravel the hoses. Hallie was standing as close as she could bear, trying desperately to see if Gerry had managed to get her mum downstairs while holding her arm in front of her face to protect herself from the heat.

One of the firefighters jogged up to Hallie, and placing his hands on her shoulders he gently pushed her back, away from the house, his face serious and full of concern.

"Is there anyone inside?" he asked.

"Yes, my mum is upstairs in the back bedroom," she said, coughing. She looked around the man, dodging from side to side so she could see the doorway, her eyes never leaving it.

"OK, stand well away and—"

"MUM!" screamed Hallie as the shape of her mum materialised and stepped, dazed, from the plumes of smoke that were flowing out of the front door. She bent over and started coughing and gulping for air. Hallie slipped underneath the arms of the firefighter and sprinted over, unperturbed by the searing heat, and grabbed her by the hands, pulling her away from the fire.

Together they collapsed on the grass, clinging to each other furiously and sobbing clean streaks down their grey faces. There they sat and watched in horror as the fire crews fought the flames that devoured their home, brick by brick.

Mum was trembling when she turned to Hallie. In a strained voice she asked, "Was it him?"

"Yes. I was there when he set the fire." Mum gasped at this and covered her mouth as a sob came from her shuddering body.

Hallie sniffed. "I'm so sorry, Mum, I tried to stop him. But he was too strong and you... you almost died," Hallie hiccupped as she buried her head in her mum's shoulder and wept. Mum wrapped her arms around her and squeezed her tightly.

"Hallie Alice Collins," said Mum after a while, as she pulled her chin up and cupped her face in her hands, "don't you dare apologise for what that terrible man did." Mum took a ragged breath. "*I'm* the one who is sorry. I didn't listen to you because I thought you were just angry about moving again but I should have taken you seriously... *I* should have protected *you*, that's quite literally my job and if I ever find that... that man," she snarled, "I'm going to do something to him that can't be repeated in front of children!" Hallie laughed at this, then Mum laughed too. They leaned their heads together and Hallie sighed with relief. They hadn't been able to stop the fire, but at least they were both safe and Edgar had been scared off by Gerry.

Once they'd both stopped sobbing Mum stood and looked at the smoking cavity that had been their home, while people in uniforms rushed here and there to salvage what they could and extinguish the embers.

"Oh sweets, I guess this means we'll have to start all over again. We'll have to move straight away too. I'm sorry," sighed Mum, sniffling.

"I don't care, Mum."

"Is this where you tell me that you don't care where we are as long as we're together?"

"Ugh, no Mum. It's not a movie," tutted Hallie, rolling her eyes. Then she laughed, "But yeah, kinda," and squeezed her mum tightly.

"I need to thank the firefighter who saved me," said Mum, wiping her face with a sooty sleeve and searching the faces of the crew. "Did you see where he went? He guided me down the stairs and he was awfully polite."

Hallie shook her head but now she understood how Gerry had managed to get Mum out without scaring her. His ability to change form had come in handy. He had really come through for her when she needed him most.

She was just wondering where Gerry had gone when Mila and her family came running over, bundled with blankets and bottles of water.

"Are you all right?" asked Mila, frowning. "The smell of the smoke woke me up and when I realised it was your house, I called 999."

"I didn't realise you were the one that called them. Thank you," said Hallie gratefully as Mila pulled a bright pink quilt around her against the bitter wind. "I'm OK, I think. Just a bit shocked."

"Well, I'm not surprised! You just survived a house fire. I'm amazed you can even speak!" Mila sat beside her on the grass and they watched the flashing lights, glowing orange embers and smoke flowing thickly into the sky.

"Mila… I'm really sorry," said Hallie, staring at the floor.

"What for?" asked Mila, distractedly looking through her backpack and pulling out a bottle of water and some wipes.

"You tried to be my friend and you were so nice and, well, I was an idiot."

"Yes, you were," said Mila, matter-of-factly, "but I don't understand why?"

"Oh, it's a long story, but really it's because I was afraid."

"Afraid of me? But I'm, like, the most harmless kid ever. I'm even scared of thunderstorms, remember?"

"No, not afraid of you," Hallie giggled, then sighed. "I've made friends at every new place I've moved to and then I had to leave them when we moved again. It hurt every single time and although I tried, the friendships just… fizzled out. Being alone was just easier. I can't get hurt that way."

"That sucks," said Mila, giving Hallie a one-armed hug round the shoulders, her huge eyes glassy in the moonlight, "but you know, I'm better than *all* those losers," she grinned. "Or… I could be if you'd *let* me."

Hallie smiled at the girl and thought that maybe she *could* have another go at making friends. But then her smile faded.

"What's the matter, Ghost Girl?"

"Well, now that we don't have anywhere to live, I have no idea where we'll end up. It might not be anywhere close to here."

"Don't you worry about that," said Mila's dad from behind them, with the same wide smile he shared with his daughter, "we have a holiday cottage going spare and it'll soon be the end of the busy season, so you are welcome to stay in it for as long as you need to get things sorted."

"Wait, what… really?" said Hallie's mum. "No, Mike, we can't ask you to do that."

"But you're not asking," laughed Mike, "we are offering. What kind of neighbours would we be if we just left you out in the cold when we've got cottages sitting empty?"

Mila grinned at Hallie and Hallie smiled back.

After a lot of hugging and much more sobbing, Mum went to speak to the police officers who had arrived shortly after the fire crew, while Mila and her family packed away their supplies and offered mugs of tea from hot flasks to the fire crew.

Hallie took a deep breath, enjoying the icy night air after the intensity of the heat. She scanned the garden and eventually saw what she had been searching for, a familiar shadow hovering by the birch trees. *Gerry.*

She checked no one was paying attention and saw them all absorbed in their tasks, then she crept away quickly. Gerry was grinning and leaning on a tree.

"Gerry, I could hug you! You did it!" cried Hallie and they performed a crisp high-five.

"It was the least I could do after making a royal mess of things the first time," said Gerry beaming.

"And how smart, saving Mum by making yourself look like a firefighter!" said Hallie, in awe of her friend. "You're amazing."

"Yes, I thought that was rather clever if I do say so myself. Not that she could see much in all that smoke anyway."

"And you can move things now… how?"

"Well, I realised that if I could change my form then maybe I could affect other things too and I just went for it. I didn't really think it would work, actually."

They stood awkwardly for a moment.

"I'm sorry… about the house," said Gerry. "Apparently I can't seem to keep them," he chuckled, sadly.

"I don't care about the house," said Hallie. "Mum would be dead if it weren't for you. *I* would be dead too."

"Well, I'd do anything for my friends," he smiled and Hallie threw herself into his chilly embrace.

"What will you do?" asked Hallie, pulling away and looking at the smoking ruin of the house as the ash floated all around them. "I don't think Mila will be cool with a ghost hanging around in one of her cottages."

"I'll stay here, of course," he said, gesturing to the house. "Someone has to make sure that good-for-nothing Edgar doesn't creep back. And if he does… well," then he stuck three slimy tongues out.

"Eww," laughed Hallie. "Thank you, Gerry. I'll come by as often as I can," promised Hallie. "Oh, and Gerry…"

"Yes?"

"Nothing *compères* to you," she grinned. Gerry rolled his eyes and groaned, then gave her a slow clap as she walked away.

As Hallie headed back towards Mila and her family she looked back over her shoulder, but Gerry had vanished.

Chapter Fifteen

The next morning, Hallie's Mum read the newspaper in the kitchen of their temporary home – one of the holiday cottages that belonged to Mila's dad – while wearing a mish-mash of clothes they'd had donated by their neighbours.

The front of the newspaper read: *Dolos Dodges Detectives!* printed in urgent black letters above an old photo of Edgar. It made Hallie angry just to see his smug face. The journalists had come out the night before to get the details of the story and they ran it the next morning 'to try and get his face in circulation', they said. Somehow, he had managed to evade capture and there was a manhunt in operation.

"Hallie," said Mum, "I spoke to the insurance people. I should get the payout soon, so we can at least go clothes shopping," she smiled.

"That's great, Mum," said Hallie, though nothing could replace her beloved vintage Ghostbusters jumper.

"Maybe you could invite Mila on our shopping spree too?" asked Mum, tentatively.

"Yeah, I'd like that," said Hallie, and she meant it. Mila had saved them by calling 999, she had already proven herself to be a more than worthy friend.

Living down the road from the old house was very convenient as it meant Mum could get started on the great rebuild and keep an eye on progress, and Hallie would be able to sneak out to see Gerry. But before the rebuild could begin, the ruins of the old house had to be demolished, and because Mum knew so many people in the building trade, she was able to book the demolition for today.

Before the demolition team arrived, Hallie had searched for Gerry, checking everywhere she could think of on the grounds of the old house, but she couldn't find him anywhere. Now Hallie and her mum stood beyond the safety fence, along with their neighbours, and watched as the house they had poured so much love into was brought to the ground with a groan and a great cloud of ash and dust.

"Oh well," Mum sighed, "time to start again. At least I get to design the house exactly how I want it this time!" she smiled.

"Ooh, can I have the biggest bedroom? With an en-suite bathroom?" asked Hallie, excited at the prospect of having a brand-new room for a change.

"I'm sorry, Hals," said Mum, hugging her shoulders, "we'll still have to sell it as soon as it's finished or POOF, there goes my profits and we'll be back to square one. We probably won't even move back in now that we're staying at the cottage."

Hallie's shoulders sagged. She looked at the rubble that was left as the dust began to settle. The demolition had been set up to make the house implode, but it had fallen mostly to the living room side, leaving the old kitchen area and cellar quite clear. She could see the floor, still intact and now exposed.

Then Hallie remembered what Edgar had said.

The site manager was chatting to Mum about the demolition. Her name was Caro and Hallie had never seen someone so excited about blowing up buildings, although she could see the appeal.

"Hey, Caro?" said Hallie.

"Mmm?"

"Could you, maybe... do me a favour?"

"I suppose that depends on what it is?"

"Can you go to where the cellar is, or was, and see if anything looks... odd on the floor? Please?"

"Odd how?" asked Caro, one bushy brown eyebrow raised.

"Umm, the floor having lumps or things sticking out of the ground. Just anything that looks like it doesn't belong there."

Caro looked at her for a long moment then nodded. "Yeah, OK. But only because your Mum is one of my favourite clients," she winked and walked off before she could see Hallie's mum blush and giggle awkwardly.

"Mum, really, is she flirting with you? I thought you had a rule that you're not supposed to date your contractors."

"We're not dating! At least not yet," said Mum with a coy smile. She saw Hallie's look of disapproval. "Oh, come on Hals, that's not fair. You're not the only one who's been lonely you know. If you think it's hard making friends as a kid, imagine how much more difficult it is as an adult. Besides, Caro is nice and it's good to have adult conversation for a change. Plus, she can talk about building stuff *for days*, do you know how exciting that is for me?" Hallie felt a twinge of guilt as she realised that she'd been so completely wrapped up in her own problems that she hadn't even thought about how Mum had been feeling. But she also felt a flicker of excitement. If Mum did start dating Caro, she might be more willing to try and stay in the same area rather than hauling them from county to county to find the best deal on a house to renovate. For the first time in a long time, Hallie allowed herself to hope.

They watched as Caro picked her way carefully among what remained of the walls and pushed chunks of charred wood and brick aside with her heavy boots and thick gloves. Then she crouched down.

"Hey, what's all this about anyway? What are you making her look for?" asked Mum.

"You'll see!"

Caro came back to the fence wearing a puzzled look. "There seems to be a strange cavity in the floor of the cellar, but we can't quite see what's in it so we're going to try and dig it out," then she grabbed a small pick and trowel from a huge portable tool chest and walked back to the rubble.

"Seriously, Hallie, how did you know there would be something there? What is it?" asked Mum, who now looked concerned.

Hallie explained what Edgar had said might lie beneath the cellar floor, what he had almost killed them trying to find and Mum's frown lifted as she turned her attention to the small crew that were now hammering away at the cellar floor.

About ten minutes later, Caro came back to the fence and passed Hallie a small, worn wooden box with iron corners and a heavy metal catch. The lid of the box was inlaid with the image of a flower.

"Is this what you were after?" she asked.

Hallie held the ancient box in her hands and then carefully lifted the lid.

"Yes," she grinned.

Inside the box, wrapped in a thick brown leather cloth, was a perfectly preserved carving of a flower.

“I can’t believe it,” said Mum, who reached towards the box.

“NO!” yelled Hallie, slamming the box shut. “Didn’t you listen to what I told you? If you touch it, it will kill you!”

“You don’t believe that nonsense, do you?”

“Do you want to try it and be proven wrong?” asked Hallie, scowling.

“I suppose not,” conceded Mum, “but this is a really important find, we need to take this to the museum.”

“OK,” agreed Hallie, “but can we do it tomorrow?”

*

That night, Hallie waited until she could hear her mum’s soft snores. Then, clutching the box, she stole out into the night and headed for what remained of Ashbone House.

She slipped through a gap in the safety fence, being careful not to trip over the mounds of broken bricks, though much of the rubble had already been taken away after the demolition. She stared at the exposed foundation of what had once been her home. The pale stone seemed to glow like a skeleton in the moonlight and the effect was quite eerie.

Gerry appeared beside her, making her jump.

“GERRY! What have I told you about sneaking up on me!”

“Sorry, I couldn’t resist it for old times’ sake,” he grinned. Then he saw the box and gasped. “Is that what I think it is?”

“Yes, it looks like awful Edgar was right after all.”

“Well goodness me,” he said as Hallie opened the box, showing him the flower carving that lay nestled within.

“Do you want to…”

“Touch it? Well, er, yes. I… I suppose so.”

“What will you do if it brings you back to life?”

"Well, it probably won't, I mean, does it work on ghosts or would I have to be a festering corpse?" said Gerry, the words spilling out uncontrollably.

"Gerry, it's OK. You don't have to try if you don't want to," said Hallie gently.

"I know, I'm sorry, it's just… I'd never thought it would be possible, so I've never even considered what it would be like to be alive again," then he looked thoughtful and a slow smile warmed his face. "Oh, but just imagine, child. A second chance, to do all the things I couldn't do the first time. I could travel again, I could learn to sing, I could do… well I could do just about anything!" He laughed, then he paused and looked at Hallie.

"But if I do touch it and I'm somehow whisked away to wherever my remains are, I ought to tell you…"

"Tell me what?" asked Hallie.

He turned and took one of Hallie's hands in a cold grip, "You are my *very best friend*, and you saved me from, well, from myself," he said, shuffling his hovering feet. "You fixed me when I thought I was beyond repair and I'll miss you, Hallie Collins."

Hallie's breath caught in her throat, "I'll miss you too, Gerry," she said with a croak as she quickly wiped away her tears.

Then he closed his eyes, reached out and touched the statue.

Chapter Sixteen

Hallie held her breath and waited for something to happen.

But nothing did.

"I guess it was just a myth," sighed Gerry, slowly pulling his hand back from the box.

"I'm so sorry, Gerry, after everything Edgar said I was so sure it would work," said Hallie as she slowly closed the box with a soft click.

"It doesn't matter," he smiled, "I'm not terribly sure I'd even fit into this modern world anyway with your telephone devices and new contraptions. Besides, I'd miss being invisible," he grinned, but something in his voice told Hallie that he was deeply disappointed. "Anyway, you should get back to bed before it looks like you've scarpered with a priceless treasure!" he laughed. "Thank you, though, for trying," he said earnestly, "it was very kind of you. It's been a long time since anyone cared about me that much."

Hallie gave him a thin smile then he said goodnight and disappeared, leaving Hallie clutching the box to her chest.

*

After an excitable phone call with Professor Cooke, the conservator at the local museum, Hallie and her mum took the Hebonas stone to the museum, along with Mila, whom Hallie had invited along.

"Hello, how wonderful of you to come, please follow me," said Professor Cooke, greeting them at the door. His eyes were kind and crinkly and he led them to his office, shuffling down the long, brightly lit corridor until they reached his room. There were tables and filing cabinets piled high with boxes and papers that were worn and faded. The walls were filled with huge pinboards covered with overlapping news articles that were yellowing and crisp and curling at the edges.

Professor Cooke cleared a small space among his things and Hallie carefully set the box down. The Professor bent down and put on some clean white cotton gloves, then he opened the lid, peeled back the leather cover with a pair of tweezers and peered at the stone. "Fascinating," he said. He opened his desk drawer and took out a large magnifying glass and looked more closely. "You said that Edgar Dolos told you about this, is that correct?" he said, still examining the stone.

"Yes, that's right," said Hallie.

"The same one that burned our house down trying to get to it," said Mum stiffly.

"Yes, that's what it said in the newspaper," said Professor Cooke. "Though they never mentioned this," he said, pointing at the stone with his magnifying glass.

"No, we found it after the fire," said Hallie, "but it's definitely what he was after. It's exactly as he described it."

"Edgar Dolos... well I haven't heard that name for some time," said Professor Cooke, shaking his head. "I thought he might be a bad egg, but I never imagined he could be capable of *that*. I'm so sorry you lost your house, how awful for you all."

"Wait, you knew him? How?" asked Hallie's mum, surprised.

"Knew *of* him, really," said Professor Cooke, standing and pushing his glasses back up his pudgy nose. "He was quite famous in archaeological circles, but mostly because of his father who was a bit of a superstar in the antiquities world. But then one of his discoveries was discredited. It turned out to be a fake and so he fell out of favour."

"What is his dad like?" asked Hallie, remembering Edgar's hurried phone call to his father. "He's still alive, isn't he?"

"Yes, I believe he is," said Professor Cooke. "In truth, he is a brilliant man, a true trailblazer, but I'm afraid he had very high expectations of Edgar and he was very vocal in expressing his disappointment in his son, who as far as I know has never made any significant finds in all his years in the field. There's nothing more disheartening for an archaeologist and so Edgar became rather bitter."

"His dad sounds a bit mean to me," said Mila and Hallie nodded in agreement.

"Now," said Professor Cooke, "tell me again what Edgar told you about the Hebonas stone, every detail."

Hallie recounted everything she could remember. Although it had been a traumatic experience, she had remembered everything he said.

"It's so strange; you know I feel like I've heard that name before but I can't quite place it." Professor Cooke took his glasses off and massaged his forehead, frowning. He began to pace across his office in slow, deliberate steps as he mumbled to himself. Hallie and her mum gave each other concerned glances. "Wait a minute!" he exclaimed, clicking his fingers, then he walked across his office and riffled through a huge pile of newspapers until he found what he wanted. He held up a newspaper and pointed to the front page which had a picture of their house engulfed in flames on the front page. Hallie's mum winced as though she had been punched.

"I'm sorry," he grimaced when he saw her reaction, "but I just wanted to check something." He quickly scanned the small columns. "That's it! *Ashbone* house," he said, looking delighted.

"Yes, that was the name of the house," confirmed Hallie's mum with a look of confusion.

"It's an anagram, you see. If you take the letters from ashbone and rearrange them, it spells hebonas. Whoever built the house probably hid it there under the foundations and perhaps they left the name as a clue."

*

They left the artefact with Professor Cooke with the promise that he would let them know as soon as he had run some tests to check the age of the carving, as well as the chemical composition to determine whether it was, in fact, infused with deadly toxins as Edgar has said. He had also promised not to touch it with his bare hands since he wanted to remain firmly in the land of the living.

"Do you want to come back to the cottage for a bit and hang out?" Hallie asked Mila as they headed back to the car.

"Yes!" said Mila, a little too enthusiastically, and Hallie grinned. It felt nice to spend time with someone who wanted to spend time with her too, someone her age at least. She was glad of a new friend, but she missed Gerry dreadfully and still expected to see him hovering in the corners and floating through the walls.

Back at home, Mila and Hallie talked excitedly about a new film coming out called, 'Day of the Ghosthunter'.

"Please come and see it with me, Mila, I promise you'll love it!" pleaded Hallie.

"But you know I don't like the creepy stuff," whined Mila theatrically.

"But ghosts aren't even that bad or scary, I should know I–" then Hallie clapped her hand over her mouth as she realised what she was about to say.

Mila lifted an eyebrow, "How exactly should you know?" asked Mila, her interest piqued.

"Uh, b-because I have read absolutely loads of books on ghosts," she felt a pang then as she remembered that all her beloved books had gone up in flames. "Anyway, it means I'm a total expert on these things, that's all."

Hallie felt a sudden chill of goose bumps on her arms and a familiar prickling at the back of her neck. She smiled before she heard the voice close to her ear.

"Nice recovery," whispered Gerry.

"Did you hear something?" said Mila, whipping her head around. "I thought I heard someone whispering." Then Mila started rubbing her arms briskly. "Ooh, it's suddenly got really cold in here," she said, shivering. "This summer has been a bust, the weather has been rubbish."

"Oh, I've probably just left a window open somewhere," said Hallie. Then she faked a long yawn, which turned into a real yawn. "You know I'm feeling pretty tired, I think I might need a nap," said Hallie, stretching her arms wide.

"OK," said Mila cheerily, "I'm not surprised after everything you've been through lately." Mila got up to leave and Hallie showed her out.

"I'll call on you tomorrow, OK?" said Hallie, leaning in the doorway.

"Yeah, no worries," said Mila, "see you tomorrow."

Hallie closed the door and then sprinted back to her bedroom. "GERRY!" she yelled as he appeared next to her, and then, aware that this cottage was much smaller than their old house and her mum could probably hear every word she was saying, she dropped her voice to an excited whisper. "*Gerry*, what are you *doing* here?"

"Sorry, I didn't mean to come, I know you'd rather I didn't, only…" Gerry hesitated, fidgeting with his bowtie.

"What, what is it?"

"Well, you remember that I lost my dear friends the night the opera house burned down? Well, I found them again!" Gerry was bobbing up and down like a buoy in choppy waters. "Hallie, dear, they want to meet you. Tonight, if you can. You are the girl that fixes ghosts after all. Can you come?"

"Gerry, that's brilliant," grinned Hallie. "Yes, of course I can come! We'll have to wait until it gets dark though so I can sneak out. I'll see you at the house, OK?"

Hallie waited until she knew her mum was asleep, her snores echoing around the small cottage, then she threw on a few more layers of clothing and left. She hated sneaking around but she knew that Mum finding out about Gerry would have much worse consequences.

Hallie walked to the spot where her old home had been and looked around the empty space, waiting for Gerry. The rubble had been cleared and only foundations remained, ready for the rebuild to begin. The site was littered with skips, diggers, stacks of timber and piles of bricks. After a few moments, she felt the air change and turned around to see the excitable ghost gesturing for her to join him. As she stepped towards him, she heard a familiar sneering voice.

"You again!"

It was Edgar.

Chapter Seventeen

Hallie fumbled in her pocket and then screeched, "Edgar, don't!" as loudly as she could. She broke into a run but stumbled on some stone chippings and he cleared the space between them in a few long strides.

"Gerry!" she called in alarm, and just as Edgar reached out Gerry appeared between them and roared, exactly like a lion, before dropping into a semi-crouch like a sprinter on the start line. Edgar snatched his arm back and then paused for a moment, taken by surprise, before snarling at the spirit, "I'm not afraid of you and your antics, GERALD SINCLAIR." Gerry's face changed in an instant as he recognised his living name.

"How on earth did you...?" he asked, bewildered.

"Oh, I know all about you," said Edgar snidely as he and Gerry began to circle Hallie, Gerry with his back to protect her and Edgar prowling like a big cat looking for a space to strike. "Yes, it took me a while to remember where I'd seen your hideous face, but then it came to me. You owned the opera house, the one I *burned down*," he said the last part with a particularly nasty look of satisfaction on his face; he was enjoying watching Gerry squirm.

"What? No, I didn't," argued Gerry, "I was just the compère."

"And then I burned down your house too," continued Edgar, gesturing at the new house.

"This wasn't *my* house, now you're really talking nonsense!" scoffed Gerry.

"You don't remember *anything*, do you?" said Edgar with a look of utter contempt. "I shouldn't be surprised; you always were a fool."

"Remember *what*?"

"Yes, you *were* a compère, that much is true, but only because you loved being the centre of attention. You owned the opera house, they plastered your pictures all over it after you died and, if the rumours are to be believed, you were one of the richest men in the country."

Gerry was listening, warily, and now and then a flicker of recognition would cross his face. Edgar continued, "Your love of the opera house was only topped by your love of fame and notoriety, and you did more and more ridiculous things to make sure you stayed in the spotlight." Hallie watched as Gerry flinched and she realised that Edgar was telling the truth.

"But not everyone loved you," he snarled, "my father for one. When he uncovered the Hebonas stone, the most precious artefact of his career, and donated it to the museum, YOU bought it from them and paid them to keep it a secret. Then when my father tried to tell the world what you'd done, you used your influence to discredit him and ended his career."

Hallie gaped. Surely it couldn't be true.

"Well, that's ridiculous," said Gerry, "why on earth would I spend lots of money only to hide it if I wanted to be in the spotlight? Answer me that!"

"That's easy," said Edgar, "you bought it for yourself so that you could be the master of life and death because you were so vain and so desperate to be loved… but you didn't think it through." Edgar made a tutting sound and shook his head disapprovingly.

"You soon realised that if the world knew of your possession, *everyone* would try to take it from you and you'd be looking over your shoulder for the rest of your miserable life. So, instead of sharing this incredible find with the rest of the world, as my father would have, you selfishly hid it beneath this sham house that you built so that no one would know of your vanity. Pathetic."

"Sham house? What do you mean?" asked Hallie, who could see Gerry wilting under the weight of the accusations.

"Oh, he never actually lived there, he was at the opera house practically all the time anyway, with his big parties and celebrity friends. No, he built it purely to hide the Hebonas stone, burying it under the cellar like he buried my father's career. He's nothing but a coward," jeered Edgar, jabbing a finger at Gerry.

Hallie looked at Gerry, his usually robust figure looking fragile now as he crumpled to the ground, just like the first time she'd met him. The Gerry that she knew bore no resemblance to the one from Edgar's tale, but Hallie could see that he remembered this version of himself and his cheeks burned with shame.

"But *I* know the truth," hissed Edgar, "and I have come to reinstate my family's name. Now, child, I came here looking for the stone but you already found it, didn't you? GIVE IT TO ME!"

"It's too late!" cried Hallie. "It's at the museum already. But it doesn't work anyway, Gerry tried it and nothing happened."

"You incompetent idiots. It doesn't work on *spirits*; it has to touch the mortal remains of the deceased."

Gerry, who had started fading in and out, moaned with grief and gave Hallie a look of complete hopelessness as she started scrambling away from Edgar, who was advancing now that Gerry had given up the fight.

"Well, I suppose I'll have to break into the museum and steal it," said Edgar, striding towards the frantic girl. "But since you'll ruin my plan if I let you go, I suppose I'll have to deal with you first," he growled.

Hallie started to run.

"Oh no you don't!" cried Edgar, who only managed to take a few strides toward her before—

"OOF!" Edgar was knocked to the ground by an unseen force.

Edgar was winded. He gulped, struggling to get his breath back, then coughing said, "Oh come on, Sinclair, it's too late for your tricks!"

"I-It's not me," said Gerry, barely visible as he flickered in his spot on the floor. As Edgar reached out to grasp a brick he was picked up and thrown, as though by an invisible hand, and landed in a dusty heap fifteen feet away from Hallie. He gasped for breath as Hallie clambered to her feet and ran to Gerry.

"Are you OK?" she sobbed as she skidded to a stop and crouched beside him.

"Oh Hallie, I am so sorry. All of this was my fault. If I wasn't such a wretched human being none of this would have happened."

"It doesn't matter, Gerry, that isn't who you are now."

They heard a grunt and watched as Edgar gradually stumbled to his feet, dazed, and then Hallie saw something interesting. The air shimmered around Edgar as though he were standing in a column of rising heat. The glimmery wall then broke off into three more distinctive figures that surrounded Edgar, who was now shivering and cursing, using words that Hallie had only ever heard her mum use when she thought she was alone.

"Gerry… is that?" Hallie began, but before she could finish a maniacal giggling sound exploded from one of the shapes. Edgar jumped, startled by the bizarre sound and then whipped his head around as a very loud sneeze and then a series of hiccups echoed around him. Edgar was tripping and twisting to find the source of the noises, but he was met with nothing but cold air. Then he caught sight of Hallie and furiously began stalking towards her. But he didn't get far before his way was blocked by the sudden appearance of an elegant woman in a luxuriantly sparkling floor-length gown.

"No, you don't!" she shrieked, almost pushing Edgar backwards with the considerable force of her voice. He frowned, confused by the apparition who then began to hiccup uncontrollably. Edgar shook his head, as though trying to deny her existence. As he began to walk around her a young woman appeared in a glitzy black dress and high heels. She wore a large white feather in her hair and danced around him laughing giddily.

"I don't think so, sweetie," she said and then launched into a sneezing fit. The sneezing was so intense that it sent shockwaves through Edgar, knocking him onto his back and throwing dust into his eyes. Edgar rubbed at his face furiously and began to stand, but before he could right himself a man's head appeared between his legs. Edgar's eyes bulged and he scooted backwards as the dismembered head started to shriek with laughter, which descended into a torrent of frenzied giggles.

Hallie could pinpoint, quite clearly, the moment that Edgar snapped. He tilted his head and grinned terribly, with a little drool escaping from between his lips which were pulled back in tight, blue lines.

"THAT'S ENOUGH!" screamed Edgar. "I am ending this NOW!" He looked deranged. His face was a violent red and spittle flew from his lips. He stood up, purposely ignoring the ghostly trio that surrounded him. He fixed Hallie with a menacing glare and marched towards her, not even acknowledging the wall of icy air that encircled him.

Edgar let out a strangled war cry and was so intent on reaching his target that he didn't hear it. But Hallie and the ghosts did.

The heavy footsteps crunched on the gravel driveway and the spirits quickly vanished as Hallie began to raise her hands and back away slowly from Edgar, who was in such a state of fury that he didn't notice the police officers gathering behind him. He didn't see the blue lights flashing silently on the unmarked police cars that were crowded in the driveway. He didn't hear them ordering him to stop or shouting a warning. But he definitely felt the sting of the taser as it hit his back and he jolted like a dying fish on the floor.

Chapter Eighteen

Hallie's Mum arrived at the old house a short while later after Hallie, sobbing, had called her.

"Oh, Hallie, thank goodness you're OK!" said her mum, running to her and enveloping her in a huge hug. She examined her face and hands gently for cuts and scratches and then hugged her again even tighter, kissing her head over and over.

Then she held her by the shoulders and looked into her eyes and Hallie knew that she'd messed up.

"I don't know what you were doing here in the middle of the night, ALONE, Hallie Alice Collins, but that was a stupidly risky thing to do," Mum sniffled. "Besides, the emergency services are going to start charging you if we keep calling them out!" she smiled, trying to diffuse the tension.

"Oh Mum," groaned Hallie, "I'm so sorry, but can we please not do this now? I'm so tired and I've got a million questions that I'm going to have to answer soon."

"Well, I've got a million more," said Mum, "but since I'm tired too, they can wait until after you've given your statement to the police. They have kindly said you can do it tomorrow morning, so they'll have time to process and question Dolos, though I don't think they'll be getting much out of him," she said, looking at the man who was staring vacantly at absolutely nothing from the police car window.

Hallie breathed out, gratefully.

"But mark my words we WILL be discussing it, young lady."

They walked back to the cottage together silently, her mum's arm slung around her shoulders, and Hallie thought that this time of night was quite nice if you ignored the flashing blue lights and police radios. The air was fresh, the streets were quiet and the night animals roamed freely.

"Look, just one question then," said Mum as they plodded wearily down the road and Hallie rolled her eyes and sighed. But she thought that, of all people, her mum at least deserved an explanation.

"Oh, go on then. But you'd better make it a good one," yawned Hallie as she rubbed her eyes.

"Who called the police? I need to thank them for saving your life," said Mum quietly.

Hallie gave her mum a clumsy smile and then pointed at herself with both thumbs, "Well look no further."

"What? How did you manage that without Edgar noticing?"

Hallie took her phone from her pocket and showed it to her mum. "I have an emergency SOS dial on my phone," she said pointing to her screen. "I've been practising switching it on without looking at my phone in case, you know, I happened to be chased by a homicidal maniac on the loose. Anyway, after the fire the Police took my phone number and put it on a watch list in case Edgar came back. I guess it worked."

Mum considered this for a moment, a lopsided smile on her face, "You know what would have been *even* smarter?" she said.

"What?"

"NOT GOING OUT ALONE IN THE MIDDLE OF THE NIGHT!"

"Yeah, point taken," then Hallie allowed herself to be guided home and dropped gratefully into bed.

The next morning, Hallie had a thorough grilling first thing at the police station where she was warned of the risks of roaming the neighbourhood alone at night when there was an arsonist out for revenge. When she eventually got home, she had an even worse grilling. Hallie told Mum that she had been 'treasure hunting' on the site in case there were more important finds which Mum seemed to only half believe, but before Mum could ask any more questions her phone chirruped.

"This isn't over," she said, raising her eyebrows at Hallie as she answered her phone.

Hallie watched as her mum's eyes widened, then she put her hand over her mouth and then she started crying silent tears.

"Mum, what is it?" asked Hallie, putting her hand on her mum's arm as she looked pale and unsteady. Hallie guided her mum to the sofa, afraid she might fall over otherwise, as she finished the call.

"Yes, thank you. Thank you very, very much," said her mum before hanging up. Mum took a deep breath, her eyes wet. "That, er, was the museum," she said slowly.

With all the excitement and terror of nearly being caught by Edgar and getting a glimpse of Gerry's wonderful friends, Hallie has almost forgotten about the Hebonas stone being at the museum.

"That was quick. What did they say?"

"Well," Mum took a shaky breath in and blew out an even longer one, "Professor Cooke said that after running their tests and putting out the feelers, an archaeologist from another, larger museum contacted them and verified that it was definitely the Hebonas stone which had gone missing years ago."

"That's brilliant!" said Hallie, brightly. "So why are you crying?"

"He said this stone is a national treasure and many people have been searching for it because of its historical significance." Mum looked at Hallie and held both her hands. "Hals, the stone is apparently incredibly valuable and… well… they are going to pay us a lot of money as a reward for finding it and returning it to the archaeological community."

"Mum… how much are they going to pay us?" asked Hallie breathlessly.

Her mum looked back at her, "Lots," she whispered and started to sob happy tears as she picked Hallie up and swung her around, hugging her tightly.

"Wait," said Hallie, stumbling as Mum put her down, "so what does this mean, for your job, for us?"

"Well… Caro has offered me a job consulting with her firm since I know so much about buildings and all," she grinned. "I wasn't going to take it since I would have so much work to do on the new house, but since I'll be able to pay other people to do all the work now, I'll be able to give up on renovations altogether."

Hallie gave her a wide-eyed look.

"So, I suppose we can finally settle here in the lovely house that I'm going to build for us with the money from the museum."

Hallie didn't say a word. Instead, she just hugged her mum tightly and sobbed with relief.

*

Hallie was lying in bed later that night, mulling over all the new information in her head when she felt a shiver creep up her left arm. She hadn't seen Gerry since the police had arrived and the ghosts had to vanish. She turned onto her side and grinned as his familiar face appeared next to the bed beside her.

"I'm so glad you came," she whispered, sitting up, "I never got a chance to talk to you about everything that happened and I don't think I'll be able to sneak out anymore. Are you OK?" asked Hallie.

"Yes, dear one. I'm all right, you know me," he said, smiling warmly, "but I do feel awful. After hearing what I used to be like, how vain and selfish..." he paused, shaking his head solemnly. He looked up at her with his face so full of regret it made Hallie want to cry, "And it was entirely my fault that you were there that night. I should have known better than to ask you to come since Edgar was still at large, but I was being selfish again. I was just so excited for you to meet my friends. But if I'd known that Edgar was creeping around I'd have neve—" Hallie cut him off.

"It's OK, Gerry. Really," she said soothingly.

"Well, it's not really. I was a terrible person and the reason you almost died... twice! I'll understand if you can't forgive me." His whole body slumped, his head hanging low.

"Gerry, what happened was Edgar's fault. *He* set the fire, *he* tried to kill me, not you. There's absolutely nothing to forgive."

"But I was so horrible when I was alive. Just a thrill-seeker. Vainglorious and arrogant. I trampled over the reputation of others simply because of my vanity," Gerry started to sob. "I'm so ashamed and I'm so terribly, terribly sorry."

"But you're not like that now. You saved my life, and who knows why you were like that," shrugged Hallie. "Maybe someone did something awful to you. Just like Edgar's dad being mean to him made him all bitter and nasty."

"You know I finally saw it," said Gerry, looking at Hallie with big glassy eyes.

"Saw what?"

"The white light."

Hallie gasped. "But you didn't go?"

"No. I expect the reason I never crossed over was because I had to face the person I had been. Maybe the Hebonas stone being found set right my wrong. But I couldn't go. Not now that I've found my friends again." One by one, three ghosts appeared at the foot of Hallie's bed. The ghosts that had saved her from Edgar.

Hallie smiled and they smiled back silently, hanging in the air. An older lady in a luxurious red floor-length gown, a young woman with a black dress and a white feather in her hair and a grinning man in a charcoal suit.

"Hallie, as it turns out, they are all as dreadfully broken as I was. Affected by the fire too, we think. Do you think that perhaps, if it's not too much trouble, you could help them too?"

"Of course," said Hallie smiling broadly, "I'd do anything for my friends."

About the Author

Nadine grew up in Devon in the era of leg warmers, cassette tapes and scary public information adverts. The world baffled her a bit and so she preferred to bury her nose in books and one day dreamt of becoming a writer herself – mostly so that she would finally know enough words to beat her Grandad at Scrabble.

However, life had other ideas, and Nadine became a secondary school art teacher instead; where she has spent well over a decade promoting exploration, creativity, and trying (and failing) not to get paint on her clothes.

After her daughter was born, Nadine was drawn to the vibrant and playful world of picture books, and although she had dabbled in poetry, blogging, and flash fiction, it was in children's literature that she finally found a home for her unquenchable urge to write.

Nadine writes smart and funny rhyming picture books and middle-grade novels that explore themes of the paranormal, mythology, and folklore; because that's what she was obsessed with growing up. She hopes to inspire the next generation of curious children who dream of things that exist beyond the normal.

She lives in Gloucestershire, surrounded by magical hills and ancient forests, where she lives with her husband, her daughter, three silly cats, and a dog with giant ears.